PRAISE FOR
ANNA STRONG, VAMPIRE SERIES

PARADOX

"Supernatural intrigue and criminal mayhem that ricochets from double-cross to double-cross. Jeanne Stein at her best!"

—*Mario Acevedo, author of the Felix Gomez vampire-detective series*

"Stein's Anna Strong is a kickass vampire, but it's her humanity that will sneak up to steal your heart."

—*Warren Hammond, author of KOP and Denver Moon*

"Anna Strong is trying desperately to wear every hat on the rack: bounty hunter, wife, mother... and the most powerful vampire in America. Her adventures are edge-of-the-seat exciting."

—*Charlaine Harris, #1 New York Times bestselling author*

HAUNTED

"Many unexpected twists and turns . . . Packed with action that is sure to chill readers to the bone."

—*Examiner.com*

"Fast-paced . . . Fans of the series will be stunned by this powerful, twisting thriller."

—*Midwest Book Review*

"Haunted offers true edge-of-your-seat drama . . . Buckle up, because megatalented Stein is heading into severely hazardous (and unputdownable) territory!"

—*RT Book Reviews* (4 ½ stars)

"Dynamic . . . Anna is what every urban fantasy heroine should be. A tough, gutsy, complex character who delivers what's promised."

—*Smexy Books*

"[Anna is] a badass, no-mercy kind of girl . . . If you want some kick-ass vampire in your life, this series is just for you!"

—*Under the Covers Book Blog*

CROSSROADS

"A kick-ass heroine readers will delight in . . . *Crossroads* will take readers on some twist[s] and turns that won't let you put this book down until the very end, and then you will be hungry for the next installment."

—*Fresh Fiction*

"[A] powerful novel . . . Stein continues to challenge her gutsy heroine, both emotionally and physically . . . Another for your must-read pile!"

—*RT Book Reviews* (4 ½ stars)

"I just love the character Anna. She has grown so much from the beginning, and I believe she is finally coming into her own in *Crossroads* . . . There were some surprises that I wasn't expecting . . . Make no mistake, Anna is growing into what she could become, and it is good to see. If you love strong female leads, then this series is for you."

—*Night Owl Reviews* (Top Pick)

CHOSEN

"With each book in the series, not only have Stein's characters become stronger but so has her writing . . . Hard-hitting urban fantasy with a hard-hitting female lead."

—*Fresh Fiction*

"From the opening chapter of this terrific series, Stein has sent her gutsy heroine on an uncharted journey filled with danger and bitter betrayal . . . In this pivotal but emotionally brutal book, skillful Stein reveals some critical answers and delivers some devastating blows. Like a fine wine, this series is improving with age. Brava!"

—*RT Book Reviews* (4 ½ stars)

RETRIBUTION

"The fifth book in the exceptional first-person Anna Strong series is a powerful entry in an amazing saga."

—*RT Book Reviews*

"Ms. Stein has a true gift in storytelling and continues to add exciting new elements to this well-built world. Retribution is an engrossing read with an action-packed story line and secondary characters that are every bit as intriguing as the heroine. This is a must-read for fans of the series!"

—*Darque Reviews*

LEGACY

"Urban fantasy with true depth and flair!"

—*RT Book Reviews* (4 ½ stars)

"As riveting as the rest . . . One of my favorite urban fantasy series."

—*Darque Reviews*

THE WATCHER

"Action fills every page, making this a novel that flies by . . . Dynamic relationships blend [with] complex mysteries in this thriller."

—*Huntress Book Reviews*

"An exciting, fast-paced novel . . . First-rate plotting."

—*LoveVampires*

"Dazzles readers with action-packed paranormal adventure, love and friendship. With many wonderfully executed twists and turns, this author's suspenseful writing will hold readers spellbound until the very end."

—*Darque Reviews*

"Snappy action and plot twists that will hold readers' interest to the last page."

—*Monsters and Critics*

BLOOD DRIVE

"Once again Jeanne C. Stein delivers a jam-packed story full of mystery and intrigue that will keep you glued to the edge of your seat! Just like [with] the first book in the Anna Strong series, *The Becoming*, I could not put this book down even for a second. You will find yourself cheering Anna on as she goes after the bad guys. Jeanne C. Stein has given us a wonderful tough-as-nails heroine everyone will love!"

—*Night Owl Reviews*

"Jeanne C. Stein takes on the vampire mythos in her own unique manner that makes for an enthralling vampire thriller. Readers of Laurell K. Hamilton, Tanya Huff and Charlaine Harris will thoroughly enjoy this fast-paced novel filled with several action scenes that come one after the other, making it hard for the readers to catch a breather."

—*Midwest Book Review*

THE BECOMING

"This is a really, really good book. Anna is a great character, Stein's plotting is adventurous and original, and I think most of my readers would have a great time with The Becoming."

—*Charlaine Harris*, #1 *New York Times* bestselling author of the Sookie Stackhouse novels

"With plot twists, engaging characters and smart writing, this first installment in a new supernatural series has all the marks of a hit. Anna Strong lives up to her name: equally tenacious and vulnerable, she's a heroine with the charm, savvy and intelligence that fans of Laurell K. Hamilton and Kim Harrison will be happy to root for . . . If this debut novel is any indication, Stein has a fine career ahead of her."

—*Publishers Weekly*

PARADOX

AN ANNA STRONG VAMPIRE NOVEL

JEANNE C. STEIN

HEX PUBLISHERS

PARADOX

Copyedits by Daniel George, Jennifer Melzer, Joshua Viola and Dean Wyant
Cover art by Aaron Lovett
Cover design by Aaron Lovett and Joshua Viola
Typesets and formatting by Ellen Hubenthal

A Hex Publishers Book

Published & Distributed by Hex Publishers, LLC
PO BOX 298
Erie, CO 80516

www.HexPublishers.com

Joshua Viola, Publisher

Print ISBN-10: 1-7339177-3-X
Print ISBN-13: 978-1-7339177-3-5
Ebook ISBN-10: 1-7339177-4-8
Ebook ISBN-13: 978-1-7339177-4-2

First Hex Edition: 2019

10 9 8 7 6 5 4 3 2 1

Printed in the U.S.A.

ACKNOWLEDGMENTS

I HAD A DIFFICULT TIME COMING UP WITH A title for this book. Mostly, I think, because it's been so long since I've released a full length Anna novel, I wasn't sure if there was still an audience for it. I've received dozens of emails asking if Anna would be back, but it wasn't until Josh Viola and Hex Publishers offered to publish it that I started thinking seriously about Anna's return.

I ultimately chose *Paradox* for the title, which is in keeping with the theme of the book. In reality, though, I could have just as easily gone with *Genesis*. In a very real sense, this is a second beginning for the series. If it succeeds at all, it will be because you, as readers, have asked for more stories. I hope you enjoy this one.

There are always so many people to thank when an idea makes it from its first creative spark to a finished book: Josh Viola and Hex Publishers, who really are responsible for my taking the leap; extraordinary artist Aaron Lovett for the cover; my Denver writing buddies, who I miss more than I can say; my family, always supportive and encouraging; Anna's friends and fans, who haven't forgotten her.

She hasn't forgotten you, either.

—JEANNE C. STEIN

ONE

DAY ONE

MY NAME IS ANNA STRONG. I'M A VAMPIRE.
Became one not by choice, but through a quirk of fate. I'm married to a shape shifter, and he has a son who is already showing remarkable powers of telepathy—early signs he's inherited his father's abilities. He's half Navajo, which is why we've decided it's important for him to spend time on the reservation with his grandparents during the school year. But it's also why I look forward to my favorite season: summer.

Frey and John-John are here with me in San Diego, my home. For eight glorious weeks, we can live as a family. Maybe not your typical family, not even your typical blended family. But as close to family as a vampire can expect. I'm grateful every day for the gift.

Still, there are concessions that have to be made. Today, for instance, Frey is taking John-John to the Wild Animal Park. Some animals become agitated in my presence, no doubt sensing the predator lurking just beneath the surface, so this will be a father/son outing. Reluctantly, I see them off, then head for my office along the coast on Pacific Highway.

I'm a bounty hunter. In fact, it was on a job that I got turned. You'd think that might have made me rethink my career choice. In reality, my abilities as a vampire make it easier. Not that my business partners are aware I'm no longer one of them…that is, strictly human.

I've got the top down on the Jag, enjoying the wind and blue sky and brilliance of the sun on the water. It's early so I don't expect my partners, David Ryan and Tracey Banker, to be in. I'll fix coffee and sit on the deck, letting the sun warm me. Thankfully, thousands of years of acclimatization have allowed vampires, whose physiology runs to cold-bloodedness, to enjoy a fine summer day just like anyone else.

And blend in with a human population that, for the most part, knows nothing of our existence.

So when I cruise into the parking lot, and see David's Hummer is in its dedicated parking space, I'm surprised. I pull into mine and go inside.

I should have knocked before barging in.

David and his girlfriend are on the deck, making out on a lounge chair. David has his hand under her blouse. Luckily, I can't see where Gloria's hand is.

"Jesus," I say, rolling my eyes. "Can't you guys find a better place to do that?"

Gloria starts to get up, but David pulls her back down.

I can guess why.

He rolls his eyes back at me. "What are you doing here?"

"I work here, remember? What if I'd been Tracey?"

I ask the question because it wasn't long ago that David and Tracey were an item. They broke up, but I know Tracey's wound is still raw.

David waves a hand. "She's gone up the coast. Taking a few days off. Which is what I thought you'd be doing, too."

"Frey and John-John are spending the day together," I reply. "I thought I might come in and catch up on paperwork."

David finally releases Gloria and she stands. She's tall, big-boobed, small-hipped, with legs that seem to start at her neck. You've seen the type. Like one of the Victoria Secret Angels, which she actually was until her acting career took off. Now she tosses her perfect mane of blonde hair and eyes me with the critical, appraising glare I've come to know and hate.

"Anna. It's been awhile. If I didn't know better, I'd say you were avoiding me."

"You'd be right," I reply sweetly. I may be the reason they're back together after an on-again, off-again relationship that started years ago, but I've made it a point to avoid seeing her.

David stands now, too, tugging his shirt down.

Jesus.

Gloria continues taking inventory. "You really should do something about your hair. I have a stylist here in San Diego who works miracles. I'll give you his card."

She pushes past me and goes to the desk. From the inside of a cavernous Michael Kors handbag, she withdraws a card. "Here. I'll go with you if you'd like. I have a few ideas."

So do I. Plenty of them. But when I don't take the card, she lays it on the desk in front of me.

David comes in from the deck and stands behind her, his hands on her shoulders. For a handsome former NFL player who could have any woman he wants, David's choice of girlfriend has always left me dumbfounded. Gloria is a narcissistic, self-absorbed bitch. Okay, she's gorgeous, and some say she's talented. And she's rich. And she and David make an eye-popping couple who turn heads wherever they go.

Still…

David picks up his keys from the desktop. "I'm going to run Gloria home. Will you hang around till I get back?"

I nod.

Gloria places her hand on my arm before following him toward the door. "Think about it," she says. "Pablo is an absolute miracle worker with problem hair. And when we're downtown, I know a fashion consultant who loves a challenge."

My teeth grind so hard, my jaw hurts. Miracle worker or not, no stylist is going to be comfortable having a client who casts no reflection in a mirror. I wait until I hear the door closing behind them before flipping the card into the trash can.

I drag fingers through my hair. It feels all right, short, curly. Is my hair really so awful? Frey has never mentioned it. Maybe I should ask him—

What am I thinking? I heave a sigh. When am I going to stop letting Gloria get to me?

The phone rings before I can answer the question.

I reach across the desk to snatch up the receiver and am

greeted by a familiar voice.

"Ms. Strong? This is—"

It's what I get for not checking the caller ID.

"I know who this is," I cut him off with a snort. "What does Chael want?"

There is just a heartbeat's hesitation before Pierre LeDoux, Chael's smooth-talking assistant, laughs. "You have a very good memory, Ms. Strong. Chael asked me to inquire if the messenger has arrived yet."

The words have barely left his lips when the office door opens. I raise an eyebrow to the FedEx delivery man and motion him over. He hands me an envelope and a tablet and points where I am to sign. I do. He sees himself out.

I heft the envelope and speak into the receiver. "I think he just did. What's this about?"

I can practically hear LeDoux nodding at his end. "Very good. Chael will be in touch after you have a chance to review the material."

And with that, the line is disconnected.

Great.

I hang up and move around to take a seat at the desk, the envelope in hand. It's one of those priority mail envelopes. When I open it and reach inside, the only thing I pull out is a newspaper article with a handwritten note attached. I immediately recognize LeDoux's flowing, precise penmanship. Chael is a powerful vampire of Mid-Eastern descent, hundreds of years old and the head of one of the worldwide vampire Council of Thirteen. He can speak English but is not proficient in writing it. For that, he relies on LeDoux, a linguist who speaks, reads, and writes a dozen languages.

I glance first at the article. It's from the *New York Times*, dated two days ago. The headline reads: *Writer Attacked Outside Restaurant*. Before I read further, I look at the note.

Anna, this woman is becoming a problem. She's headed to Los Angeles to continue her research. Chael wants to meet with you to discuss what's to be done about her. He'll be in contact.

The note is signed with LeDoux's usual flourish.

I sigh. If Chael is involved, this cannot be good. Especially for the woman. I pick up the article, settle back in my chair and begin to read.

———————◆●◆———————

John-John comes home with a stuffed giraffe almost as tall as he is. I meet him at the door and sweep both him and the toy into my arms. "What in the world is this?" I ask, laughing.

He gives me that look. "You know what this is, Anna. It's a giraffe! And we got to feed one at the Wild Animal Park. Do you know what they eat?"

I set him down and Frey steps beside us, encircling my waist with an arm. "Why don't you tell us?" he says, leaning close to peck my cheek.

John-John windmills his arms in excitement. "They eat leaves. From the top of tall trees. And they eat hundreds of pounds of leaves a week. Hundreds of pounds!"

His enthusiasm makes me smile. One of the things I love about having a child around is that sense of wonder I lost long ago…and never thought I'd find again. As a vampire, I can't have children. Marrying Frey and being step-mother to John-John is an extraordinary gift.

"Okay, son, time to wash up for dinner," Frey says.

John-John grabs his toy and skips off.

"Could he be any cuter?" I sigh.

Frey shakes his head in amusement. "He has his moments. We've only been home two days, though. The halo will wear off."

I put my arms around Frey's neck and pull his face close. "What about your halo? When will it wear off?"

Frey glances at his watch. "Right about John-John's bedtime," he says with a grin.

"I can hardly wait."

We disentangle and Frey follows me into the kitchen. I can't eat food, but Frey and John-John do. When they're home it's fun to play Suzy Homemaker, a role I'm not accustomed to. Tonight I've fixed lasagna with salad and bread. Well, to be honest, I bought the lasagna at a local deli. Garlic and I don't get along.

Frey breathes in appreciatively. "Smells good." He pulls the cork on a bottle of wine and pours us two glasses. Handing me one, he says, "So, what did you do today?"

I take the glass and sip before answering, "Well, nothing of interest at the office. Except for this…" I hand him the envelope from Chael.

Frey lifts an eyebrow as he takes the envelope and looks inside. He withdraws the article and the note.

"Chael."

His tone says it all. This vampire has never been one of Frey's favorites. There is a natural enmity between shifters and vampires, but Frey's feelings go far beyond what's natural. Chael was once determined to get rid of me, and made several attempts on my life. He and I have since managed a truce, but Frey's instinct to protect me makes it hard for him to trust Chael. They are barely civil to each other.

Now Frey frowns as he reads, first the note, then the article. When he finishes, he looks up at me. "Is this real?"

"I guess." I pull the lasagna out of the oven and place the pan on a trivet. "I admit I'm curious. I did a computer search on her—she's a New York Times bestselling author. Writes fiction—paranormal fiction. Vampire fiction. Could it be a coincidence that she was attacked from behind by someone who tried to bite her neck?"

Frey looks dubious. "It could simply be a publicity stunt," he says. "The article says she has a new book about to be published."

"And she's working on a non-fiction piece," I add, setting out plates and utensils. "About the supernatural underground."

Frey shakes his head. "Not the first time someone's claimed to be ready to—" he makes air quotes with his fingers—"'expose what creatures live amongst us.' Probably won't be the last either."

"And yet Chael is concerned enough to bring this to my attention."

Frey clucks his tongue. "Chael looks for any excuse to

intrude in our lives. This is just his latest." He narrows his eyes and shakes his finger. "He's sweet on you. And he thinks I'm an unworthy consort to the Chosen One. The next thing we know, he'll be at our front door."

I grin and plant a kiss on his cheek. "Doesn't matter what he thinks. I say you're more than worthy. I plan to show you how worthy later tonight."

"Yippee," Frey growls, pulling me close.

"I hope John-John tired himself out at the Wild Animal Park."

"I did my best," Frey replies. He takes one of my hands and slides it down between us. "God, I missed you."

I grin up at him. "I can tell."

John-John is in bed and Frey and I are enjoying a glass of wine on the deck from our bedroom. The ocean sparkles and froths under a sliver of the moon. The sky is full of stars. Our lounge chairs are so close I feel the warmth of Frey's skin where his arm comes in contact with mine. It sparks the sweet ache that's part lust, part hunger. Frey will let me feed from him tonight while we're making love. It's the cement that binds us even closer than marital vows.

Frey stirs beside me. He's placed his glass on the deck and stands, offering me his hand. "Ready?" His voice is a rumbling whisper, full of promise.

I take his hand and let him pull me up. I press myself against him and he leans in for a kiss. His passion sparks my own. Breathless, I lead him into the bedroom. In a heartbeat, we're out of our clothes. Frey backs me to the bed, his hands and lips busy. I cling to him, surrendering. When he enters me, the world explodes in a whirlwind of sensation. And when I find his neck and begin to feed, we are lifted to new heights.

Sex and blood.

For a moment in time, I'm alive again.

TWO

DAY TWO

FREY AND JOHN-JOHN ARE WITH ME, COMING to say hello to David before we head out for a day at the beach. John-John runs into David's open arms.

He picks up the boy and swings him around, John-John squealing with delight. When he sets him back down, John-John says, "We're going to the beach. Come with us."

"I'd love to," David replies. "But I have a job this morning." He winks at me over John-John's head. "Some of us have to work."

"Tracey here?" Frey asks.

David shakes his head. "Nope. Seems I'm going solo on this one."

Frey takes a step forward. "Need any help?"

I turn and raise an eyebrow. "You want to go with David on a job?" I glance at John-John. "What about the beach?"

Frey shrugs. "You go ahead with John-John." He glances

at David. "We shouldn't be too long, should we?"

David turns to the desk and picks up a flyer. "Not for the two of us. The skip is a white collar embezzler. Ran out on his bail in New Mexico. He's been spotted up the coast in Del Mar."

The details sound alarmingly familiar. Several years ago, David and I were after a white collar skip who turned out to be a vampire. It's how I was turned. I put a hand on Frey's arm. "White collar doesn't mean harmless," I remind him.

He knows the story. He's also aware that David knows nothing of the consequences of that night, nor does he know Frey is a shape-shifter. It's not that I don't think Frey can't handle himself. It's that if the job turns bad, I'm afraid he might have to reveal himself.

Frey seems to be reading my mind. "I promise not to do anything dangerous," he says. "I'll leave the heavy lifting to David."

David flexes a well-defined bicep. "Yep. Heavy lifting is my specialty."

John-John, who very well may have been reading my thoughts, speaks up. "I think Dad can take care of himself." He sounds reassuring and very grown up.

"Okay. Guess I'm outnumbered." I stand on tiptoes and give Frey a quick kiss. "Just be careful. No heroics."

He squeezes my hand. "I'll leave heroics to David, too."

David gathers up his keys. "Let's go, then. We should be back by three." He motions Frey ahead of him toward the door and when I'm the only one who can see what he's doing, he opens his jacket to show me that he has his Glock holstered at his waist. He winks and follows Frey out the door.

If that gun is supposed to put me at ease, it doesn't.

John-John finds a box of donuts by the coffee machine. David must have picked them up on his way to the office. He looks at me with hopeful anticipation.

"One," I say. "You can have one."

John-John takes the box to the desk. It takes two seconds of thoughtful deliberation before he picks a jelly-filled, glazed concoction. My mouth waters as he dives in. Fetching napkins from the corner coffee station, I take a seat opposite John-John to vicariously enjoy his pleasure.

I so miss the simple things.

John-John is scrubbing the jelly off his face and I'm at the coffee station putting the donuts away when the office door opens.

Anna, John-John's voice is in my head. *A vampire just walked in.*

I whirl around, ready to attack.

John-John, Chael says, opening his mind to John-John, too. *I've looked forward to seeing you again. We met at your grandparent's home in France.*

John-John nods. *I remember.*

Now I have no reason to think Chael would harm Frey's son, but all the same, I place myself between the boy and Chael. "You can speak out loud," I tell him. "John-John knows what I am."

"Obviously," Chael replies.

"I know why you're here," I tell him. "What I don't know is why you are so concerned."

Chael takes one of the office chairs. "I'll tell you."

I open the desk drawer, find some blank paper and a pencil. "John-John, why don't you go out on the deck and draw me a picture?"

John-John takes the paper from my hand. *I'll be right outside if you need me.*

Chael chuckles as we watch John-John take a seat on the deck outside, facing into the office.

"He's obviously inherited more than Frey's shape-shifting abilities," he says. "He's also inherited his protective gene."

"One of the reasons I love them both."

Chael shakes his head. "Yet you don't need anyone to protect you, do you?"

My eyes drift to John-John. "We're a family. Protecting each other is what families do."

Chael sighs. He's of Middle Eastern descent with dark, thick hair and soulful black eyes. He's about five-foot-eight, wears his bespoke designer suits with easy elegance. I don't know how old he is, in human years he looks fifty-ish, but I'd guess he was around when the first crusade launched to wrest Jerusalem from the Muslims. He wasn't always a friend. I can't be certain he's one now, but he was there for me when my mother died not too long ago and I've come to begrudgingly trust him.

Now he sighs again. "I wish it didn't take a crisis for me to seek you out," he says. "Always, it's the same."

"Crisis?" I sniff. "I hardly call this a crisis."

"Then you don't understand what's going on."

I narrow my eyes. "Please, then, enlighten me."

Chael crosses one leg carefully over the other, smoothing the crease in his slacks. "You read the article?"

I dig it out of my purse.

"You have it with you?"

"Frey figured you'd be visiting us sooner or later. I thought I'd be prepared."

"Janet Carlysle, the author, is very well known and very popular. Her fans number in the millions. One of her books, *The Dead Among Us*, has sold twenty-five million copies worldwide. It was made into a TV series that garnered even more fans."

I shift impatiently in my chair. "I could have found all this out by Googling her. As you obviously have. Not all of this was in the article."

"Up until now, her works of fiction have elicited very little attention from the vampire community. Just another mortal putting her own spin on what she believes the vampire existence to be. But this last book, what she calls a prelude to her nonfiction work, contains some items that hit close to home."

"Such as?"

Chael fastens those intense black eyes on me. "A Chosen One. A powerful vampire who heads the Council of Thirteen. Who determines the destiny of all vampires." He pauses. "Who also lives in San Diego."

"How could anyone outside the vampire community

know all that?" I ask.

He raises his shoulders. "No one should." He reaches into the inside pocket of his jacket and withdraws a paperback. "I think you should read this. The only thing she doesn't seem to know about is your private life. In her story, you are living in the mansion of a master vampire you vanquished. You spend your days hunting rogue vampires."

All things that sound very familiar. When I first became vampire I was "mentored" by a very old, powerful vampire. He turned out not to be a friend at all, but a manipulative enemy. I killed him in self-defense, and "inherited" his wealth—which included a mansion in La Jolla that sits unoccupied to this day. I also worked for a while for "The Watchers", the underworld equivalent of a police force that hunts down and eliminates rogues whose reckless behavior threatens to expose vampires to the world.

"Too many coincidences," I admit.

"And now, there's this *non*-fiction book she's proposing." Chael shakes his head. "I think you should find out who's feeding her information before she goes too far."

"Got any ideas how I'd go about that?" I ask sarcastically.

"You're not serious." He waves a hand around the office. "Isn't that your business? Isn't that how you track down bail jumpers in this job you're so fond of? You have resources the average person doesn't."

"Okay," I concede. "Where does she live?"

"Close," he answers. "Los Angeles. It's on the back cover of her book. Think of this as another skip to hunt. Finding her close acquaintances, places she frequents. Trail her for a while. She's bound to lead you to her source eventually."

"*Eventually* is the key word," I say. "John-John and Frey are with me for the summer. I plan to spend as much time with them as I can. I don't intend to take on a wild goose chase just because some writer happened to come up with a plot that bears some similarities to my existence."

"Similarities?" Chael huffs. "Come on. Well—" He stands up. "I've said what I came to. Read the book. I placed a card in it where you can reach me when you're ready to act. In the meantime…" He waves good-bye to John-John. "I'll leave you to your beach time."

With that, he strolls out the door, as casually as if he'd stopped by for nothing but a friendly visit.

I stare after him. But Chael's visits are never so simple. He's up to something.

Shit.

And I'm being dragged into whatever it is along with him.

◆●●◆

John-John is playing at the water's edge with two other kids it took him about a minute to befriend. They're building sand castles. Every once in a while I tune into his thoughts. He's engrossed in the intricacies of castle engineering and how wet to make the sand.

I return to the book.

I'm sitting on a beach chair under an umbrella. One of the benefits of being a "modern" vampire is that I have the advantage of the thousand years or so it took vampires to acclimate to sunlight. No relegation to dark coffins during the day.

Janet Carlysle's book is open on my lap. It's not badly written, but Chael was right, there are too many similarities between Elizabeth, Janet's protagonist, and myself. Even the physical description is too exact to be merely a figment of Janet's imagination. Elizabeth is described as five-foot-seven (check), with honey blonde, naturally curly hair (check), and blue eyes (check). I know that description fits millions of people, but the details of her life are almost identical to mine. How she became a vampire (attacked outside a bar, check), identified as vampire by the doctor who treated her in the hospital (check), being taken under that doctor's wing (check). The fact that the doctor became an enemy that had to be eliminated (check).

I turn the book over and look at the author's picture. Not a glamour shot. She's dressed in an open-neck shirt, sitting against the hood of a car, a dog at her side. She looks to be thirty, hair drawn back from an average but friendly-looking face. Her bio says she lives in the hills above Los Angeles with a menagerie of animals. No mention of a family.

I return to my place in the text. I'm about halfway through when a shadow falls on the book and I look up.

"You're back!"

Frey, dressed in a pair of cutoffs and a tee, sits down on the blanket beside me. "Guy didn't even put up a fight."

"You sound disappointed."

He leans forward and plants a kiss on my forehead. "A

little, maybe." He strips off his tee shirt and his eyes scan the beach until they find John-John. "He looks like he's having fun."

But there was something in Frey's tone when he said he'd been a little disappointed. I turn his chin to face me. "Are you all right?"

He places his hand over mine. "Why do you ask?"

"Our life has changed a lot since we've been married," I say. "We have John-John. You're on the reservation most of the year, teaching school. Are you having a hard time adjusting to 'normal' life?"

He laughs. "If you're asking if I miss the trouble we used to get into—" He pauses. "Well, maybe. We had a lot of adventures together. Most of them I wouldn't care to repeat. But the rush… Adrenaline is addictive." He notices the book in my lap. "What are you reading?"

I turn the cover over so he can read the title. "This is the book Chael is concerned about?"

I nod.

Before we can discuss it further, John-John spies his dad and runs to greet him. "Come on, Dad," he says. "Help us build a castle."

Frey lets himself be pulled to his feet. "That 'normal' life you think I'm having a hard time adjusting to? There are trade-offs."

I watch husband and son walk to the water's edge. Even as I wish our life was always as uncomplicated as it is today, the book in my lap seems proof that *normal* and *uncomplicated* will never be permanent conditions for us.

THREE

DAY THREE

I WAIT UNTIL JOHN-JOHN IS IN BED TO TELL Frey about Chael's visit.

We're in our favorite deck chairs, watching the moon rise over the water and sharing a good bottle of French wine from my family's estate.

Frey shakes his head. "I told you Chael would be in touch. This was quick even for him." He gestures to the paperback sitting on the bed. "What do you think? Is he right to be concerned?"

"Maybe. I admit, there are a lot of similarities to my history in what she writes. She has a vampire contact, I'm certain."

"Do you think it's Chael?"

I look at Frey in surprise. That hadn't even occurred to me. On the other hand… No. "It's not Chael," I say. "What would he gain by ratting me out and then telling me about it? Convoluted, even for him."

"Maybe." Frey takes my hand and pulls me up. "But *convoluted* is Chael's middle name. He's here in San Diego. I'm overwhelmed with joy."

I reach up and tangle my fingers in his hair, bringing his face close to mine. "Let's forget Chael," I say. "We only have two months. Let's make the most of it."

———— •●● ————

The next morning, the three of us are sitting at the breakfast table, planning our day. We've narrowed our choices to a trip to Laguna Beach or up to the Cuyamacas. I'm at the coffee maker ready to refill Frey's cup and cast my vote when a cell phone rings in the bedroom.

I tilt my head and listen. "It's yours," I say to Frey.

He pushes back from the table. "Be right back."

But he isn't. It's ten minutes before he rejoins us, his face drawn and serious.

"What is it?" I ask, alarm spiraling at his expression.

"What's wrong, Daddy?" John-John goes very still. He's reading his father's thoughts.

Something I can't do. "Frey, tell me."

Frey puts his arm around John-John's shoulders. "It's his grandmother. She's had a stroke."

"Grandpa wants us to come back," John-John adds. His eyes fill with tears. "He thinks she's going to die."

"No, son." Frey gathers John-John into his arms. "He didn't say that. But she is very sick and he thinks she'd feel much better if you visited."

"Then we need to go." I grab up my cell. "I'll get the jet ready. We can be in Monument Valley by lunchtime."

Frey shakes his head. "You don't need to go," he says. "Stay here and we'll be back as soon as we can." He sends John-John to his room to pack and turns to me. "You know how things are on the reservation. John-John's grandparents are very old fashioned. They are still mourning the death of their daughters."

"I'm the outsider who contributed to their death."

Frey takes me in his arms. "I know it wasn't your fault but they can't be objective. It's still too soon."

John-John's mother was collateral damage during my visit to the Navajo Reservation with Frey to see a Shaman that held the secret to mortality. While there, we became aware of a scheme to flood the market with fake Navajo artifacts. John-John's mother had nothing to do with it, but her sister did. The two were together when the sister's partners decided she could not be trusted. They caused the car accident that killed them both.

I wasn't involved with the scheme or the accident, but I was with the investigation.

Guilt by association. I couldn't blame them. They lost both their daughters, one of which was their grandchild's mother.

I sigh. "I understand, but you just got here." Dreams of our summer together fading before my eyes.

"I promise, we'll be back as soon as we can."

He kisses me. I hold on to him until I can bring myself to pull away. "Get ready. I'll call the pilot."

He lets go of my hand. I watch him disappear around the corner and heave a breath.

Our life will always be complicated. Sometimes I wish I wasn't always right.

I'm back from the airport. I unlock my back door and toss the keys onto the kitchen counter. Frey and John-John are on their way to Monument Valley and I'm alone.

Again.

When I call the office, David answers on the first ring.

"It's me. Anything going on?"

"Here?" He sounds surprised. "I thought you were taking the day off."

"Change of plans. So if you have a job…"

"Frey want to come along again?"

"No. I want to come along." I fill David in.

Silence follows. "Wow. He wasn't here long."

"He'll be back as soon as he can."

"Why didn't you go with them?"

I can't blame David for asking the question, but since he doesn't know what I am, what Frey is, or how complicated our time in Monument Valley is, I struggle to come up with an answer.

"Oh, before I forget—" David saves me by speaking first. "You got a call this morning. From Chael. He's in town. Did you know that?"

David met Chael at my wedding in France. "No. When

did he call?"

"About an hour ago. He said he tried your cell but it went right to voicemail."

I pull my phone out of my jacket. I'd forgotten I turned it off. When it powers up, Chael's message is there along with one from David.

"Did he say what he wanted?"

"Said he wanted to meet you at The Flash at noon."

I glance at my watch. 11:30. "Guess I'd better get going then. But you didn't answer me. Anything going on today?"

"Nope. We have a meeting with Duke this evening, though."

Duke is one of the bondsman we work with. "What time?"

"Five. His office."

"See you then."

David rings off.

I snatch up my keys.

I'm never thrilled to meet with Chael. He was in Monument Valley, too, when John-John's mother was killed. I don't consider him a friend now, but at that time, it's not an exaggeration to say that we were enemies. We've come a long way toward mending those fences, but I don't think I'll ever completely trust him. I'm sure he wants to know what I'm doing about that author.

The sun has burned off the morning fog, drawing beachgoers to the shore in droves. Joggers, skateboarders and roller skaters make maneuvering even the boardwalk a challenge. A leisurely fifteen minute walk morphs into a thirty minute game of human dodgeball.

By the time I join Chael, my irritation level has entered the red zone. He looks at me and signals the waiter. Pointing to his own glass, he says, "Jameson. Neat. And one for the lady." Glancing at me again, he adds, "Make hers a double."

"Isn't it a little early?"

"Not from the expression on your face." He looks behind me. "Where are Frey and John-John? I thought they'd be with you."

I don't want to go into details with Chael. Monument Valley isn't a good memory and it hadn't ended well for him, either. My family isn't any of his business.

"Why did you want me to meet you?" I ask, avoiding the subject and keeping my thoughts carefully hidden from his prying mind.

He shrugs. "Trouble in paradise? He's been home, what, five minutes?"

My drink comes, and I gulp it, saving Chael from finding my hands around his neck.

"Have you read the book?" he asks then.

"About half of it."

"What do you think?"

"If you mean we are in imminent danger of being outed by this hack writer, I don't agree."

He arches an eyebrow. "Really? After all the similarities between you and her protagonist? Even down to the light curly hair on your head?" His tone doesn't disguise his impatience. "What will it take to convince you we need to talk to this woman? Publishing your address? Photos of you, Frey and John-John?"

"She couldn't do that. She'd open herself for an invasion of privacy suit."

"But the damage will be done. You have gone to great lengths to hide your true nature from those closest to you—David, your family."

"Who's going to believe vampires exist? She'll look like a delusional crackpot."

Chael is quiet for a moment. "I can see you don't take this seriously. Maybe that will change when she comes after you."

My head snaps up, my eyes skewer his. "Why would she do that?"

Chael reaches into a jacket pocket and withdraws a photograph. "Maybe you should see this."

I look down. The photograph is of Culebra, my Mexican friend who provides vampires a safe feeding place in his bar in Beso de la Muerte. People who are aware of the existence of vampires offer themselves as hosts in exchange for money or, sometimes, sex. Culebra is standing outside the bar smoking a cigar. "Where did you get this?"

"From a reliable source close to Janet Carlysle's publisher. He also happens to be a vampire and a very good friend of mine. He told me about her next project, a nonfiction 'exposé' on the secret life of vampires. She's already set her sights on you—I think this photo proves it. It's only a matter of time before she catches you going to Culebra to feed."

I look away. It's true. When Frey is gone, I go to Beso de

la Muerte to feed. "How could she know?"

Chael shakes his head. "My source is trying to find out. But I took the precaution of arranging for Carlysle to have another unfortunate—"

"You were responsible for the first attack?"

"Don't look so surprised. I was hoping to nip this in the bud before it got any further. It didn't work. This time—"

I bang my fist on the table, interrupting again. "Are you crazy? You're confirming what she's trying to prove! That vampires exist."

Chael blew out an exasperated breath. "This time it won't be a vampire." He speaks as if explaining something to a slow child. "This time it will be a mugging."

"How is that going to discourage her?"

"She can't write another book," he says softly, "if she's dead."

FOUR

I WANT TO THINK CHAEL IS KIDDING BUT I CAN see he isn't.

I narrow my eyes and put steel in my voice. "You can't kill her. She's an innocent."

"An innocent?" Chael's tone is sharp, incredulous. "You don't really believe that, do you?"

"Chael, she hasn't done anything to put us in danger. Has she turned anything in to her publisher besides this picture?"

He shakes his head. "There are a couple of others, but so far, no pages. That's why we have to act quickly."

"Oh, God." I press my palms against my eyes. "Call it off."

"What?"

"Call off the attack."

"Too late. It's happening tonight," he says. "Then we can forget all about her. I can go back home. You can have your magical summer with Frey and John-John. Isn't that what you want?"

"What I want," I tell him, pushing myself back from the

table, "is for you to take out your phone right now and call off the attack."

"What then? What's going to stop her?"

"I am." As soon as the words are out of my mouth, I see something shift in Chael's expression. "You son of a bitch," I snap. "This is what you wanted, isn't it?"

He smiles. "I have a plane waiting for us at the airport. We can be in Los Angeles in an hour."

I glare at him. "Of course we can."

———●●●———

I expected Chael's plane to be even larger than my jet so it's quite a shock to have him lead me to a small twin-engine Beechcraft that looks like a Honda Civic with wings. It's an even bigger shock after he consults with one of the ground crew, waves him off and opens the cabin door himself, sliding the airstair into position. He motions me to board.

I look around. "Where's the pilot?"

"You're looking at him."

I stare. "You're the pilot? You know how to fly?"

He chuckles. "How hard can it be? I've watched a dozen YouTube videos. It's really simple. Besides, we're vampires. If we crash, what's the worst that can happen? Unless the plane explodes in mid-air, we'd just brush ourselves off and …"

The look on my face must mirror the horror I feel. After a moment, Chael bursts into laughter. "Relax. I have my license. Want to see it?"

I don't know what surprises me more. The fact that Chael

is a pilot or that the man who, until a few months ago, led me to believe he didn't speak any English is now cracking wise.

What else is up his finely tailored sleeve?

He motions me ahead of him up the steps. "You better not be kidding me about that license," I say.

Chael laughs. "You'll find out, won't you?"

The cabin of the Beechcraft holds four over-sized leather chairs. Chael heads for the cockpit and indicates with a jab of a thumb that I'm to sit beside him. I'd been in my own plane's cockpit, but always as a visitor. This time I was to sit in the co-pilot's seat. A new experience.

Chael shows me how to buckle in and adjust the headset. He starts the engines. I listen to him chatter with the tower and his take-off instructions. A uniformed ground crewman approaches to remove the chocks from the wheels and signal that Chael is next in line to take off. Chael taxies into position and a minute later, we are airborne.

Very different from the thrust and pitch of a jet, the Beechcraft feels like a butterfly rising on a cushion of air. Chael sets our course, then relaxes back in his seat.

"What do you think?" he asks.

"Very smooth," I reply.

"For local travel, you can't beat a Beechcraft."

He sounds like a commercial.

We are traveling so close to the ground, I can see the faces of people in the cars on the freeway. I have to admit, this is far less hassle than what I go through to get the jet ready for an hour's flight to LA. By the time I contacted the pilot, filed a flight plan, and the crew prepared the jet, we could have driven there.

"Do you know where Janet lives?" I ask after we've been airborne a few minutes. My voice echoes through the headset.

He nods. "Got her address from that friend who works for her publisher. I have a car and driver waiting for us at the airport. He'll take us to her house."

"What makes you think she'll see us?"

Chael smiles, but it's not warm. "Oh, she'll see us. She thinks we're coming to interview her for a magazine article. Her publisher set it up."

"You've thought of everything, haven't you?" I reply with a snort. "Any idea of what we're going to say when we're face to face?"

"Good choice of words," Chael replies dryly. "I'm all for showing her what we're capable of."

"We are not scaring her," I say. "Got that? We need another way to convince her we're too dangerous to play around with."

Chael shakes his head. "You're mistaken if you think a soft approach will work. She's already been attacked and that didn't dissuade her."

I sink back into the seat. I hope I can convince her to drop this project. I wish I had the ability to compel her to forget, like TV vampires. All they do is gaze deeply into a human's eyes. Unfortunately, that option isn't open to me. Vampire to vampire, we can influence each other's minds, but vampire to human, not so much. A major design flaw.

Chael's voice breaks into my thoughts, getting landing

instructions from the tower at Burbank Airport. We've arrived. I gaze down at the rabbit warren of buildings and crowded streets that cover every square mile of Los Angeles. City of Angels.

A misnomer for sure.

The Burbank Airport is a small, intimate airport, a respite from the chaos that is LAX. Chael is directed to a place to park the Beechcraft. He shuts off the engines and we deplane. A ground crewman approaches and after a brief conversation, Chael signs off on the flight and we are directed to the terminal. He is conversing telepathically with his driver, who directs us where to meet him. He stands next to a big Lincoln Town Car, and as we approach, opens the back passenger door and waits until we are inside to take his place behind the wheel.

He has an air of comfortable familiarity with Chael, which makes me think he's one of the vampires in his tribe. There are thirteen tribes in the vampire world—Chael is the leader of the Middle Eastern cabal. I am the leader over all of them. Luckily, I don't have to sit on a throne or conduct meetings. Vampire society is decentralized. Each tribe governs itself. The thirteen only gather for a watershed event—the last was my assuming the position of the "Chosen One."

I hope there will never be another.

Chael introduces me to Abbas, the driver. We have to converse telepathically because Abbas doesn't speak English. Vampires have their own version of Esperanto—thoughts are universally understood regardless of one's native language.

Still, I'm skeptical. "Does he really not speak English?" I

ask Chael with a suspicious glare. "Or is he like you? Able to speak English when it suits him."

Chael grunts. "No. He really does not speak English. He's only been in this country a few weeks. I brought him in to learn from my assistant, LeDoux."

"So how is he going to know where to drive us?" I ask.

I get my answer when the engine turns on and a GPS recites directions—in Arabic.

The Hollywood Hills are part of the Santa Monica Mountain range. Most people don't think of Los Angeles as having a mountain range. It's certainly not like the Rockies or the Sangre de Cristo Mountains. No peaks over fourteen thousand feet. No peaks over six thousand feet for that matter. The Hollywood Hills are a kingdom hidden in plain sight from the city of Los Angeles. Gorgeous views above the smog reflected in pricey real estate.

We cruise along the city streets encumbered only by red lights and the occasional stalled car. We hit the Hollywood Freeway. This is why I hate driving in LA. No matter the time of day, freeway driving adds an hour to most commutes. I grind my teeth in frustration as it takes us forty minutes to travel the two miles to our exit.

Chael remains quiet during the drive. He may be conversing with his driver for all I know. His thoughts are purposely closed off to me. My own thoughts are with Frey and John-John. Selfishly, I hope John-John's grandmother is recovering and that they'll be coming home soon. I'll call Frey as soon as I'm back home.

The address we're heading to is off Bronson Avenue. The houses become bigger and grander the farther up the side of the hill we go. Finally, our turnoff takes us to Hollyridge Drive and then to Hollyridge Loop. When we pull up to a gate, my eyebrows jump.

"Just how much does this chick earn on her books?" I ask Chael.

"I believe her last contract was for seven million."

"Seven *million*? I've never heard of her before."

Chael cocks an eyebrow. "How many vampire books do you read?"

He has me there. I shrug. "We're in the wrong business. Think of the book *we* could write."

The driver pulls up to the speaker and Chael gets out and announces our presence. A buzzer sounds and the black wrought iron gates swing open. The only thing missing is a trumpet fanfare.

Janet Carlysle's home is a typical 1920's Mediterranean red-tiled roofed mansion set back from the road by a winding, tree-lined driveway. The chauffeur stops at the top of a circular driveway and Chael and I climb out. Everywhere we look, flowering shrubs and leafy bushes crowd the house. She must have a hell of a watering bill in drought-prone Southern California.

Chael precedes me up broad stone steps to a front door set under an archway of brilliant red Mandeville Vines. We ring a bell that chimes with a harmonious melody that echoes through the house. I look over my shoulder while we wait and admire the view. From this distance, the City of Angels nearly looks like it. I imagine the view at night is spectacular.

The door opens. I turn around.

I expect a maid or butler. Instead, the author greets us with a wide, welcoming smile. She would. She's expecting a reporter. When she sees us, the smile loses its brilliance.

As if she recognizes what we are or who.

She recovers. Bids us in with a sweep of an arm.

We follow her through a bright foyer into a living room. Vaulted ceilings and floor to ceiling windows reflect sunlight onto white overstuffed furniture and polished dark wood floors. It's professionally decorated. I know because there's nothing personal in the room. Even the granite bowl set in the exact center of a low coffee table and the fringed throws placed strategically over the arms of the chairs and sofa are like props on a movie set. Janet Carlysle might be rich now but she wasn't always so. She's turned her home into something copied from Architectural Digest instead of a reflection of her personality.

Janet is the only piece out of place on this chessboard. She asks us to sit down and when Chael and I take our places on either end of the sofa, she pushes an ottoman over so that she is right in front of us. She's dressed in loose fitting Target jeans and a San Diego Padres sweatshirt. Her auburn hair is piled on top of her head, not in the casual, arty way so popular nowadays, but knotted in a lopsided bun and secured with a chopstick. No make-up, not even lipstick, relieves the pale wash of her complexion or plays up her one exceptional feature—eyes the color of spring grass.

If she was expecting an interview, she obviously didn't go out of her way to dress for it.

Maybe you don't need to when you've just sold a book for seven million dollars.

While we're getting ourselves settled, I feel her eyes on me. She hasn't said a word.

Finally, she says, "Wow. I got your description right, didn't I?"

FIVE

HUNCH CONFIRMED.

"Have we met?" I ask.

"No."

No? That's it?

Chael glares at her. "You know who we are?"

She's not looking at Chael. Her eyes are on me. "I know who *she* is. You must be her friend. Maybe her bodyguard. You don't look very intimidating."

I have to swallow a laugh. She's pretty gutsy for a mere mortal in the presence of two vampires.

Chael doesn't think it so funny. "Not merely her bodyguard or her friend," he sputters. "I am the head of—"

I stop him with a hand on his arm. *No use giving her more information,* I tell him.

He backs down with a glare.

I turn and ask, "Who do you think I am?"

Janet crosses her arms and hugs her chest. "Why are you asking me? You've read my book or you wouldn't be here.

I know who, and more importantly, *what* you are. You're a vampire."

She says it without a bit of trepidation or equivocation. I find myself staring. I could deny it, argue she must be crazy to suggest such a thing, but her absolute faith in her words is obvious.

"Where did you get that idea?" I ask.

"I did my homework," she replies. "It took me a long time to find a real vampire who was willing to talk with me. He gave me just enough information to point me to you, Anna, before…"

"Who is this so-called vampire?" Chael asks sharply.

Janet shakes her head. "I won't reveal his name."

Chael shifts beside me, irritation sparking off him like flames. *We could make her tell us. We're alone with her. We could get the name of the traitor and end this now.*

I put my hand on his arm again. *Relax. No violence, remember?*

I turn back to Janet, she's watching us with wide eyes. "You can communicate telepathically? That's so cool!"

I sniff. You wouldn't think it so *cool* if you knew what Chael was thinking. "Let's assume you're right. And we're vampires. Why aren't you afraid?"

"Why should I be?" she counters. "I mean no harm. I know you don't want to be exposed. I only wrote to get your attention."

"And this non-fiction book you've proposed?"

She waves a hand. "Insurance. I figured if I made it known

I was planning to expose vampires as real, it would bring you to me. And it did."

Irritation at her attitude was beginning to make Chael's take on this situation more palatable. She acts like this is the most mundane of conversations. Maybe shaking a little sense into her *would* do some good.

"Janet, I'm confused," I say. "You believe we are vampires, and yet, you aren't the least bit afraid. You're either incredibly brave or incredibly stupid. My friend here thinks we should kill you and be done with it. That would effectively eliminate your threat to expose us if we were vampires."

Janet shrugs. "Sure. You could kill me. But you can't really believe I didn't take precautions after I was attacked." She peers at me. "Were you behind that?"

I shake my head, not letting on that the vampire behind it is sitting beside me on her couch.

"No matter." She waves a hand. "Everything I've learned is in a safe place. In the event of my death or disappearance, it will become public. Including, I should warn you, the security footage of you entering the driveway today. Coupled with the information I put in my book, that should be enough to let the world know just who you are."

"Your book also makes you look like a nut case," I remind her. "You really think anyone will take you seriously?"

We could still make her disappear, Chael says. *Along with the security footage. With the proper groundwork, it could look like she went on a research trip. A few emails from her phone to her agent or publisher and it could be weeks, even months before anyone gets suspicious.*

For the first time, uncertainty flashes on Janet's face. She's suspicious of our ability to communicate telepathically—that obviously surprised her. Maybe her informant wasn't as forthcoming as she thought.

I let another moment pass to deepen her misgivings. I stand. "We're going now. Take time to consider how far you want to push this. You aren't in too deep yet. You should be aware, though, that there are others out there who aren't as reasonable as I am."

Chael rises, too. "Stick to fiction, Miss Carlysle. It's safer."

Janet jumps to her feet. "Wait. Don't you want to know why I'm doing this?"

"It doesn't matter," I snarl.

It's the first time I've shown hostility and she cowers.

Chael, though, smiles and leans toward her. "I'd like to know," he says. "What is it you want?"

Janet holds out her wrist "It's simple. I want you to make me like you are. I want to be a vampire."

I could imagine her saying…money, power, access to the vampire community, maybe even to become a host.

Actually wanting to become a vampire was not one of them.

Not in the top twenty.

I stare at her, mind reeling.

Chael's face flashes, eyes yellow, teeth bared. "Let me do it, Anna," he growls.

The ferocity of his remark snaps me to reality. I know only

too well what Chael is thinking. He's not hiding it from me. He'll drain her, not with the intention of bringing her back, but of killing her.

Stop it, Chael. I won't let you kill her.

It's what she wants, he insists. *She's asking for it.*

She's asking to be made like us, I correct him. *Not to be drained and left to die.*

Janet is watching Chael but showing no fear, not even at seeing Chael's vampire face. She looks hopeful, optimistic.

"I don't know what to say," I tell her. "You know we're vampires but look at Chael. That is the true face of the vampire. Why would you want to be turned into something like that?" Chael stiffens beside me, *No insult intended. You know what I'm doing.*

He grunts.

Janet smiles. "Are you kidding? Who wouldn't want immortality? A perfect body? Eternal beauty? The chance to be accepted into the most exclusive club in the world?"

"Club?" I echo, aghast. "You think being a vampire is like membership in a country club? I thought you were crazy. Now I know you are."

"Come on, Anna," Janet returns my sneer with a scathing glare of her own. "You're telling me you haven't found perfect freedom being a vampire? You have a private jet, a mansion in La Jolla, which sits vacant, by the way, so I know there's a story there." She glances at Chael. "And interesting friends, like this one."

"So this is about material things?"

Janet sniffs derisively. "Look around. I already have more money than I can spend in one lifetime."

"Then what?"

"Does it matter? Isn't it fun to be able to communicate mentally? Read each other's thoughts." She glances at Chael. "Must be a terrific advantage in bed."

I give her the old fish eye. "Chael and I are not lovers," I say archly. "Far from it. There's more to consider than the fun you can have in bed. You need human blood to survive. Have you thought about that? Not goat's blood or pig's blood. Human blood, right from the source."

"Oh, I know that." She waves my concern aside like an irritating insect. "You go to Beso de la Muerte to feed on humans who are paid to be hosts. They enjoy it, too. So no need to try to scare me into thinking I'd be turned into a killing machine. I know better."

Chael is shaking his head. "This has gone far enough. Who is your source?" he roars.

Janet jumps. "I told you. I won't say."

"Why didn't you ask *him* to turn you?" Chael snaps. "Why come to us?"

"I couldn't," she says simply.

"And why is that?"

Janet lowers her eyes.

I'm just as curious as Chael about Janet's vampire source. "Chael asked a legitimate question. Why *couldn't* you ask your vampire friend to turn you?"

No answer.

"Janet, I'm getting impatient. Answer the question or we're out."

"I planned to ask him," she says finally, "but he died."

"*Died!*" Chael exclaims. "What do you mean he died?"

It's obvious Janet doesn't want to say anymore. I lean forward. "Tell us." It's not a request.

She sighs. "He was supposed to meet me one night in Griffith Park. Truth be told, I did intend to ask him. When I arrived at the park, he was waiting for me. We started to walk and —" Her voice drops. She swallows hard and continues. "I don't know how it happened. One moment we were talking, the next, he collapsed with a stake in his chest. All I felt was a cold draft, like a gust of frigid air blowing past. I watched as he…dissolved."

I'm speechless. Not only have I used all the reasons I can think of to dissuade her, but she actually saw the death of a vampire and she's still looking at me like a kid asking for a puppy.

I switch my gaze to Chael. *Someone must have found out what she was doing. Any ideas who?*

Not a clue, he answers. *I'll put some people on it.*

I know he means vampires. I nod and turn back to Janet, pulling out the last arrow in my quiver. "Have you thought about your family? Do you realize how it is when everyone you love is dying around you and you're left alone? Vampires cannot form attachments to humans because they're forced to watch as they wither and die. Your parents, your siblings, your lovers—"

"I repeat," Janet snaps. "Look around. Do you see pictures of family? Of lovers? I've been alone in the world ever since I was a teenager. I don't care about anyone but myself. I'd make the perfect vampire. No attachments, human or otherwise."

Are you ready to give up? Chael asks. *Can I kill her now?*

SIX

MY CELL PHONE BUZZES. I GRAB IT OUT OF MY
jacket pocket, see it's David and put it to my ear. Anything to
distract from the ridiculous scenario unfolding in front of me.

"Anna? Where the hell are you?"

As soon as he asks, I remember. We have a meeting with
our bondsman. "Shit." I glance at my watch. Four forty-five.
"I'm in LA."

"LA? What are you doing there?"

I release an exasperated breath. "Long story. Can you stall
Duke?" I look over at Chael and ask, *How long will it take us
to get back?*

If we leave right now, at least an hour just to get to the airport.

Great. "David, I won't be back before six-thirty at the
earliest. You go ahead. You can fill me in later. He probably
wants to talk about a job, right?"

There's a moment of dead air. David says, "I'm not sure.
I think he would have told me over the phone if it was. He
said it was important so I'll go. Come to the condo when you

get back—"

"Will Gloria be there?"

David groans and I can see him rolling his eyes. "Are you ever going to get over it?"

He means, am I ever going to get over how much I dislike his girlfriend. It's doubtful. We have history, but David loves her and he is my partner. "It's better that she and I avoid each other. I'll call you tonight when I get back."

"Okay. You are coming back tonight, right?" David hesitates a moment, then asks, "You still with Chael?"

"Yes to both." When I look up, both Chael and Janet are staring at me, obviously having followed my end of the conversation. "I'll talk to you soon."

"Why do you still have a day job?" Janet asks after I've slipped my phone back in my jacket.

"A very good question," Chael says.

"Why wouldn't I?" I counter. "I like what I do. I like getting bad guys off the street."

"Isn't it alleged bad guys?" Janet says.

"Look." I glare at her. "We're not here to discuss my life. We're here to discuss this ridiculous notion to make you a vampire. It's not going to happen. My suggestion is that you stick to fiction. If you want to write vampire novels, be my guest, but stop using me for your inspiration. I've been patient today. If I have to come back, it won't be such a friendly visit."

Janet squares her shoulders. "That's it? You don't care that I can expose you and your friends?"

I take a step closer and lean into her. "Do you really

think the vampire community is going to allow you to shine a spotlight on us? You saw what happened to your contact. You should be smart enough to know that was a warning to you, too."

Her expression hardens. "You aren't scaring me," she says. "I'm not bluffing. I'll write the book. And I'll go on every talk show I can, and I'll name you and your friends in Beso de la Muerte. A lot of people may think I'm crazy, but not everyone will. Some sharp investigative reporter will start dogging you and sooner or later, you'll do something to give yourself away. You won't be able to help it. And then—"

Chael snaps back into vampire mode. With a growl, he grabs Janet around the neck. *She has to go, Anna. You know it's true.*

He lifts Janet off her feet and shakes her.

I expect Janet to scream, tear at Chael's hands, or beg him to let her go.

She doesn't. Her eyes are not on Chael. They're on me. As if she knows I won't let him go too far. She hangs limp, waiting, letting herself be shaken like a rag doll.

Part of me wants to let him finish it. I don't know how else to handle the situation, but the human part of me knows I can't let him do it. I've only been able to adjust to being a vampire by knowing I'm capable of retaining my humanity.

I place a hand on Chael's arm. He glances at me, then slowly lowers Janet until her feet touch the floor. When he releases her, she crumples into a heap, drawing deep, noisy drafts of air that morph into a coughing fit until she catches her breath. There's no fear in her eyes. Still no fear.

I kneel down so our faces are level. "You have to let this go, Janet. You've stumbled on something dangerous. I won't be able to protect you if you persist."

Janet has both hands at her neck, rubbing the bruises darkening her skin. Her head is down, her shoulders slumped. Did I finally get through to her?

She's silent for several minutes—whether because Chael's shaking has rendered her physically unable to speak or because she's trying to find the words to concede defeat. I can't tell.

I hope it's the latter.

When she lifts her head, I see the answer in her eyes. She straightens her shoulders, tugs at her clothes. The glare she directs at me is still defiant. "You'll have to kill me," she says.

Chael grunts. *She's as stubborn as you.*

I rock back on my heels. Time to take a different tack. I stand up and reach a hand down to her. She eyes it warily, but takes it and lets me pull her up.

"I'll have to make arrangements for you to meet my friend in Beso de la Muerte before we do anything else," I say.

I feel Chael stiffen. *What are you doing?*

I ignore him. "There are certain realities you should face if you're serious about this. I wasn't given that chance before I turned. Come to my home in one week and I'll take you."

Janet looks suspicious. "How do I know this isn't a trick?"

"You don't. Use the next seven days to get your affairs in order."

"You sound like you're not sure I'll return."

"Things change when you become vampire. You need to stay away from people who have known you for a while until you get the hunger in control."

Janet nods slowly. "Okay. I'll see you in one week."

"I assume you know where I live. You seem to know everything else about me."

She nods again. "Isthmus Court in Mission Beach. The ocean side."

I want to roll my eyes in frustration but I remain stoic. "I'll call you when I've made arrangements."

She grabs my arm. "How can I reach you if I need to?"

I look down at her hand and up at her. She drops my arm. "I'll call you," I say again.

She opens her mouth to say something else but the look on my face must give her second thoughts. Her mouth snaps shut and she nods.

I gesture to Chael and we head for the door. Janet doesn't follow us. When I glance back, she's sitting on the couch, staring out at the garden.

I wonder what she's thinking.

If she becomes a vampire, I'll soon know.

———◆●●◆———

As soon as we're out the door, Chael jumps. "What the hell are you thinking?"

"Relax. I know what I'm doing. I have a plan."

Abbas is waiting at the car, passenger door open. We climb into the back.

"Every time you tell me to relax, I get nervous," Chael says when we're once more on the road. "I get even more nervous when you say you have a plan. A plan you're blocking me from reading. What is it, Anna?"

My head falls back against the cushioned leather seat. "You haven't met Culebra, have you?"

Chael shakes his head.

"He's an interesting character. Runs the bar in Beso de la Muerte. If anyone can show Janet the down side of becoming vampire, he can. I'll ask him to make sure she sees only the low lifes who come to be donors. The druggies who'll do anything for a few bucks. The bikers who insist sex be part of the package. She doesn't strike me as being particularly worldly, in spite of her tough act."

"There's a big flaw in your plan," Chael says. "What if she's not going to get her fix at Beso de la Muerte? What if she wants to strike out on her own and find her own sources? Once she's turned, we may never see her again."

He's right. Any destruction she leaves in her wake will be on me. "You got a better idea? I'm open to any suggestions."

"I already told you my suggestion. Kill her."

"Not an option." I sigh. "I've never turned anyone. I'm not sure I know how to do it."

"If it comes to that, I'll tell you," Chael says. "Let's hope it doesn't."

It's close to eight when I finally get back home. I know I

have to call David, but first I put in a call to Frey. The news is no better this evening than it was earlier. John-John's grandmother is still in critical condition. I speak to my stepson for a few minutes and can tell from his voice he's trying to be brave. When Frey gets back on the phone, I want to cry.

"I should be there," I say. "For John-John."

"I know," Frey says, his voice soft. "But there wouldn't be anything you could do—"

"Except remind everyone that John-John's mother is dead because of me."

Frey lets a heartbeat go by before saying, "Not everyone feels that way. I don't. John-John doesn't."

"I miss you."

"I miss you, too."

The moment stretches until it's time to say goodbye. I've never felt lonelier.

I sit on the edge of the bed and stare out at the ocean. It takes all my will to place the next call when I really want to crawl into bed and forget about today. Maybe dream of being with Frey.

David picks up right away.

"Do we have a job?"

"In a way."

I hear him say something sotto voce to Gloria, who is no doubt leaning on his shoulder to catch every word. I picture her naked and panting.

"Tell your girlfriend to start without you," I say snidely.

"Jesus. You two. Do you want to know what Duke said

or don't you?"

"I'm all ears."

"He wants us to track someone down for him."

"Nothing unusual. What's the guy wanted for?"

"Nothing yet. Seems he absconded with half a million of Duke's money and he wants it back. He hasn't told the police. He wants this handled in-house."

I don't like the sound of that. We'd done one other "personal" job for Duke and the consequences still haunt me. "What happens when we find him?"

"We bring him back, deliver him and the money to Duke, and collect a nice fat fee."

"Then what? What's Duke going to do to him?"

"Didn't ask. Don't care."

I draw in a quick, sharp breath. "What do you mean, you don't care? You forget what happened last time we did Duke a favor? I ended up killing someone. A dirt bag, maybe, but I killed him." And was almost exposed as a vampire, though that's something David doesn't know. "I don't want this guy ending up in a landfill."

David clucks his tongue. "It's different this time. I think the guy is a distant relative. I doubt he'd kill him."

Right. The other guy had been Duke's abusive son-in-law.

I'm quiet for a moment, and David says, "Are we in or are we out?"

"Sounds like you've made up your mind."

"It's a big payday. Low risk. Legit. Two, three days at the most." He adds, "Anna, this is our business. We can't ignore big money when it comes our way."

I sigh. What else can I do? Sit around thinking about the absurd situation with Janet, about how I miss Frey and John-John? At least if I work this with David, I can control what happens when we catch the guy. If it turns ugly, I can get the money back to Duke and let the guy disappear.

"I'm in."

"Good. We'll get started tomorrow."

"Good night, Anna," Gloria interrupts, having taken the phone from David. "He and I are getting started right now."

The phone clatters.

Before the call drops, I hear Gloria's high-pitch squeal.

SEVEN

DAY FOUR

I WONDER IF I'M EVER GOING TO ACCEPT GLO-ria as David's—I have a hard time even saying the word—*lover*. What if he marries her?

My stomach turns at the thought.

I get ready for bed and take a glass of wine out to the deck. The ocean is calm under a starry sky. I wish my mind was as calm. My thoughts swirl like the wine in my glass. I sink into a deck chair.

First, Janet. I'll have to go see Culebra as soon as I can. I imagine Janet will not be patient long. She'll expect to hear from me sooner rather than later.

Then there's Frey and John-John.

My fantasies about the summer Frey and I would be spending together quickly dissolve into the cold reality that they may not be back before John-John returns to school. Maybe thinking we can make a long distance marriage work is just wishful thinking. I know how important it is to Frey that John-John retain links to his heritage. Maybe it's time for me to think seriously about moving onto the reservation.

I take a swallow of wine.

What would I do there? How would I be received?

I drain my glass and push myself up. Tomorrow may be a better day. The prospect of what Duke wants us to do, though, casts doubt like a dark cloud casts shadow. Duke, like all bail bondsmen, is money oriented—it's the nature of his business. What idiot would steal from one? Even a relative would realize he couldn't get away with it.

There's a car parked in David's parking space when I pull up the next morning. Not his Hummer. A new Tesla Model S. My shoulders bunch. If Gloria is inside…

But she isn't.

David is alone, at the computer, mug of coffee at his side.

Exhaling with relief, I ask, "New car?"

"Like it?"

"It's about a third the size of the Hummer. What prompted the change?" I walk over to the credenza to pour a cup of coffee for myself.

David shrugs. "The Hummer was not only a gas hog, but left a huge carbon footprint."

I do a double take. Carbon footprint? A phrase David would never use, much less care about, unless it had been fed to him. I could guess by whom.

Shaking my head, I take a seat across from him at the desk. He glances up. "How are Frey and John-John doing?"

"There's no change in John-John's grandmother's condition."

"They won't be coming home soon?"

"Unfortunately, no."

He drops his eyes back to the computer screen. "I think I have a lead on Duke's nephew. His ex-wife lives in Del Mar. It was a nasty divorce. If we tell her he may be in trouble, she might be willing to let us know where he is."

"If she knows. If it's that easy, why didn't Duke contact her himself?"

"Duke wants to distance himself from this." David presses a button and the printer buzzes to life. It spits out a piece of paper. He grabs it and stands. "Let's take a ride up the coast. I'll drive."

I follow him out of the office. At the car, David pauses.

"What?" I ask, reaching for the passenger door handle. My fingers scrabble ineffectively against the side of the car. The door handle is there, but it's flush against the door.

I look back at a grinning David and he's just standing there, remote in hand. He holds it up, pushes a button. The handle rises from its perch against the side of the car.

"Very cute," I grumble, slipping into a passenger seat. My foot bumps against a box. I heft it up and read what's printed on the top.

He puts the car in drive without so much as a button to push or key to turn. It's so quiet, it's spooky. "Boy, when you go green, you don't fool around."

The car has more tricks than a circus magician. David touches a screen and a map pops up. He speaks an address and the GPS springs to life. We're soon on 5, heading north.

I settle back in a seat that seems to melt around me. "How much did this, imposing example of modern technology set you back?"

David sniffs. "If you have to ask, you can't afford it."

Right.

My expression must trigger his defensive mechanisms because David shoots me a narrow-eyed look. "Might be about time for you to get rid of that gas-guzzling tank you drive."

I sit up straighter in the seat. "My Jag is a classic."

"Sure it is. And how many miles to a gallon of premium does it get?"

I can't think of a comeback to that. I cross my arms over my chest. Time to change the subject. "Where does the ex live?" I ask.

David shakes his head to let me know he's on to me but does point to the screen. The address is on El Camino Real.

"Contentious divorce or not," I comment, "she did pretty well for herself if she lives in that neighborhood."

David raises an eyebrow. "I did a little digging. Kitty Del-Monico is fifty. She had money of her own before she married Duke's nephew, Howard. He managed to go through most of it before she got wise and cut him off. The divorce came not long after. He tried to get his half of what was left, which wasn't much by that time, but there was a pre-nup. He left a string of women and gambling debts, which probably explains why he embezzled from Duke. His uncle gave him a job when he was at his lowest, but family loyalty couldn't compete with the temptation of a cash business." David shakes his head. "It was a dumb move."

His words echo my thoughts from last night.

We hit traffic just south of town. It's Del Mar Fair time. The queue made a twenty minute drive, drag to forty. Finally, we're past the fair ground's turn-off and continuing into town.

The exit to El Camino Real sends us up above the beach and the city and into the gentle tree-lined hills surrounding it. Kitty DelMonico's house turns out to be one of the older homes in this rural section of Del Mar. It's modest compared to other multi-story luxury estates surrounding it, a sprawling one-story shake-shingle house with a tile roof fronted by a large horse corral. We spy a woman in the corral brushing a large bay mare tethered to the fence.

"Does she know we're coming?" I ask David as we pull into the driveway.

"No. Thought it best to catch her off guard."

We haven't attracted her attention, the result of the electric car's ability to run silently and the headphones she's wearing as she works. We approach the corral and when she catches David out of the corner of her eye, she jumps.

David holds up a hand as she sweeps the headphones off her head. "Sorry. Didn't mean to startle you."

I've purposely hung back. Don't want to rile the horse. I'm hoping she'll step out of the corral and come to us.

She's eyeing David. At first I think it's because most women look at him like that—a big guy, ruggedly handsome. But there's something more to the gleam in her eyes. She tilts her head "You're David Ryan. The football player."

A flush of pleasant surprise creeps up his face and widens David's smile. It may not happen as often anymore, but he still enjoys when someone recognizes him from his glory days.

Kitty DelMonico ducks between the corral fence rails and holds out her hand. "I'm so happy to meet you."

She's an attractive fifty, trim in jeans and a loose-fitting blue cotton shirt, honey blonde hair pulled into a pony tail. David takes her hand. "You have a good memory. It's been ten years since I played."

I clear my throat and they both turn to me.

David drops her hand and gestures back to me. "This is Anna Strong. My business partner."

She turns that warm smile on me, "Business partner, huh? What kind of business?"

I let David field the question since Kitty has already turned her attention back to him. She has the natural, no-make-up-needed kind of complexion that makes women envious. Her eyes are wide and her mouth generous. I imagine in her twenties and thirties she was a knock out because, if I didn't know her age, I'd never guess fifty. I'd also be willing to bet the blonde hair is natural since it's laced with strands of silver that enhance its shine.

David takes a piece of paper out of his pocket. "We're looking for your ex-husband, Mrs. DelMonico."

A bit of warmth drops from her smile. "Why?"

He hands her the paper. "He was a witness to an accident and this insurance company hired us to find him."

A very good ruse and one we use often. I imagine he handed her a letter of introduction typed on the letterhead of an insurance company with a name ambiguous enough to sound legitimate.

"A witness?" She scans the paper before handing it back to David. "I haven't heard from him for over a year. Something I can't say I'm sorry about." She turns back toward the fence and picks up a walking stick I hadn't noticed. "Come to the house with me."

David refolds the letter and slips it into his pocket. "You sounded surprised we would be looking for him. Any reason for that?"

When she starts out, it's obvious in her shambling gait that she's not as physically fit as her appearance first suggests. As we follow her, she speaks to us over her shoulder.

"Howard is bad luck," she says. "He's more likely to be the cause of an accident than a witness to one."

David's eyebrows rise as we exchange a glance.

Kitty's house is cool and dark. She crosses a foyer into a room outfitted as a combination office/parlor—large desk in the center, bookcases along the walls, a group of worn, leather furniture clustered in front of a fireplace. She goes to the desk and sinks into a chair, opening one of the side drawers.

After a moment of rummaging, she holds out an envelope. "This may be of some help."

David takes it. He holds it out to me and I can see a name and address scrawled on the front. "Is this a relative?"

"Better," Kitty says, with a smile. "Howard's bookie."

EIGHT

BACK IN THE CAR, I ASK DAVID BEFORE HE CAN ask it of me. "What do you think she meant about Howard more likely being the cause of an accident?"

We're back on 5, heading north again. The address on the envelope is in Los Angeles. David's fed it into the Tesla's GPS and we're humming along—literally.

"Do you think it has anything to do with her limp?" I ask.

David is quiet a moment, contemplating an answer, I expect.

"I didn't find anything in my research on her," he says at last, "to explain her infirmity. Maybe I should have dug a little deeper." He shoots me a sideways glance. "So what were you and Chael doing in LA yesterday? You never mentioned."

"Visiting a friend," I answer.

Seems harmless enough until David follows up with, "What friend? Who do you two know in Los Angeles?"

I can't come up with an answer. David has known me so long, it won't do to make up a name. I go for the bigger lie.

"If you have to know, we went shopping."

"You and Chael went shopping." He snorts and shakes his head. "*You* went shopping. In LA. Chael, maybe. But you? Except for the day you got married, I've never seen you in anything but jeans." He narrows his eyes. "If you don't want to tell me, just say so. You don't have to make up a ridiculous story."

"Ridiculous? I could have been shopping for Frey. Or John-John."

"Were you?"

I open my mouth to snap back but arguing will just prolong the interrogation. I change tactics. "Where is Howard's bookie located?"

"Right here," David answers, pulling off the interstate.

Howard DelMonico's bookie was operating out of a warehouse block in a seedy part of LA. Same city, maybe, but a world away from Janet's neighborhood. I don't think there's another place in the U.S. where "skid row" is marked with its own boundary sign. The bookie, Harry Sullivan, has an office a stone's throw from the famous sign on San Julian Street.

We pass the doorway twice before we realize the scratches over the door jamb were actually numbers.

"Should we knock?" David asks. He adjusts his Glock then smoothes his jacket over it.

"We'd probably be the first," I reply, grabbing the door knob and giving it a twist.

The door swings open and David and I each take a step sideways before peering inside.

The precaution is unnecessary. It's empty. It's a big square room littered with betting slips and beer cans. Marks in the dust on the floor indicate where a desk once sat. A wall-spanning whiteboard covers the rear. The light bulbs had been removed from a tarnished brass fixture in the middle of the room. Other than some wires dangling from a bracket in the ceiling corner, there's nothing else.

"He's been gone a while," I remark, rubbing a foot in the dust.

"Looks like he took everything with him," David says. He points toward the ceiling. "Including a surveillance camera and the light bulbs."

I take a desultory look around. "What now?"

But before he can answer, we're startled by a rustling sound, loud and insistent.

"Where's it coming from?" I whisper.

David unholsters his gun and moves toward the rear of the office. He examines the back wall, peering intently at what looked like nothing more than a standard whiteboard. With a finger to his lips, he points to a barely discernible outline along the perimeter of the whiteboard. He runs his fingers over it, pauses at a point about waist high, and pushes.

A section of the board releases, swinging outward.

I'm just behind David, ready to pounce if anything runs out.

Nothing does.

David lowers his gun and takes a step forward.

"Be careful," I hiss. "You don't know what's in there."

He sticks his head inside, then turns back to me. "It's

a tunnel."

I join him. "To where?"

He shrugs. "Only one way to find out."

I'm a vampire. I'm not supposed to be unnerved by anything, but the prospect of stepping inside a cobweb strewn, dirty, damp tunnel makes my cold blood run even colder.

"You lead the way."

David grins and slips by. I'm happy to let him forge the trail. The rustling we heard earlier must've come from packing material strewn on the ground. What disturbed it is not in evidence. As soon as we take a dozen steps into utter darkness the door behind us snaps closed.

"Great," I mumble. My eyes already adjusted to the dark but the door closing is like a punctuation emphasizing that we now may be trapped.

It takes an instant before we've both drawn our cell phones and the tunnel is flooded with light.

"What is this?"

David shrugs as we find ourselves in the middle of an underground bunker. It must be fifty feet across, ten feet high, and constructed of concrete bricks. One wall is stacked floor to ceiling with wooden crates. More packing material litters the floor. Three walls look solid, the fourth has a door. I push it—it opens to an alley that runs the length of the building. I let the door close behind me and turn my attention to the crates.

"What do you suppose is in those crates?"

David is whispering, though I'm doubtful there's anyone

around to hear. My vampire senses detect no sound other than our own breathing. They do, however, detect the odor of decayed flesh.

I cross the floor and peer between the slats of a crate at eye level. "Looks empty."

David joins me and reaches up to pull one of the crates off the stack. It lands with a crash.

"This one's not empty," he says grimly.

No. It's not. A human hand lies curled at our feet.

———•••———

By the time the cops come, it's well past six in the evening. A detective, who we recognize, arrives to take our statements. Contrary to popular opinion, not all cops hate bounty hunters. In fact, we'd worked with this detective, Phil Connolly, before. He's just this side of forty, a little pudgy, with the dark, serious gaze of a cop who's seen too much. We told him who we were looking for when we stumbled on the hand.

"Sullivan hasn't been around for a while," Phil tells us. "Wouldn't be surprised if that hand turns out to be his. Word is he's gotten on the bad side of some pretty rough people."

David raises an eyebrow. "Care to elaborate?"

"Care to tell me why you were looking for him?"

"He's not a skip," David replies. "We were hoping he'd give us some information about someone who is."

Connolly runs his fingers through a crown of thinning brown hair. "If he's not wanted for something, I'd say you've reached a dead end with this one."

His pun is not lost on us.

Connolly puts his notepad into a jacket pocket. "I don't see any reason for you two to hang around," he tells us. "If we find anything concerning your bookie, I'll give you a call."

David and I shake hands with Connolly and start back through the tunnel to the deserted office.

Connolly calls after us. "Ryan, is that your Tesla outside?"

David turns and nods.

"Sweet ride. I think I'm in the wrong business."

NINE

DAY FIVE

WHEN WE GET BACK TO SAN DIEGO, DAVID drops me off at the office so I can pick up my car. We agree to meet the next morning at eight and plan our next strategy to find Howard DelMonico. It's after ten by the time I pull into my driveway.

The message light on my landline blinks. Since no one important has this number, I figure it can't be anything urgent. Tired from a long drive, I ignore it and turn in.

I've got a cup of coffee in my hand when I get around to checking voicemail.

The first call is a hang up—10AM

Second call—ditto—11AM

Third call—an irate voice barks a message. "You'd better not be ignoring my calls," Janet Carlysle says. "I'm ready to come to San Diego anytime. I can be there by midmorning tomorrow. Call me back."

Jesus. I hadn't given her a telephone number. This was exactly why.

I punch in her number. I don't even hear the phone ring once before it's snatched up. "It's about time," Janet says. "When should I come?"

I inhale slowly to modulate the irritation out of my tone. "How did you get this number?"

"It's listed online," she snaps back.

It is? I make a mental note to have this line disconnected as soon as I hang up.

I can hear Janet exhaling impatiently into the phone. I purposely let a long moment go by before I say, "Janet, I told you I'd call you when everything is ready. I have a day job, you know, I haven't even had the chance to let my contact know you're arriving. I need time to set things up."

"If you think you can put me off indefinitely…"

The vampire flares. "Listen to me. I will let you know when I want you to come, do you understand? If you dare show up before I'm ready, I'll turn you over to Chael and believe me, you won't like the way he deals with you."

There's a long moment of silence. "Okay." When she replies this time her tone is much softer, much more acquiescent. "Sorry. I'm just very anxious to start my new life. I have a lot of plans…"

Plans? That doesn't sound good. But at this point, I'm still convinced that between Culebra and me, we'll be able to talk her out of her insane desire to become vampire. I soften my tone, too. "Give me three or four days to wrap up a job I'm on. Trust me. I will be in touch by the end of the week."

"I have your word?"

Is she kidding? If you can't trust a vampire's word, whose word can you trust? "Yes. You have my word."

The call quietly disconnects.

Shaking my head, I rinse out my coffee cup and head for the garage.

How do I get caught up in these things? Now, with everything else, I have to make time to head south to see Culebra. On the way to the office, I put in the call to my service provider and have that damned land line disconnected.

———◆●●◆———

David is on the phone when I arrive at the office. He waves me to the desk and I take a seat, listening to both sides of a conversation I can follow thanks to vampiric hearing.

"Duke, are you sure you don't know anyone else who'd have a line on your nephew? So far there's been no action of any kind on his bank accounts, no plane ticket bought in his name, his car was found abandoned in Chula Vista, and the lead his ex-wife gave us was a dead end."

Maybe literally, I mouth to David, thinking of what Connolly said yesterday. David nods.

Duke sighs into the phone. "I wish I had something else to give you. He's got to be somewhere. Five hundred thousand can buy a lot of cooperation but anyone I know who could make someone disappear, denies being contacted by him."

"Would they tell you if he had?" David asks.

"I doubt they'd lie to me," Duke replies. "In the long run, my services are far more valuable to them than one score."

The second line rings and I grab it on my side of the desk. It's Detective Connolly. "Got some news," he says. "The forensics team found the remains of two individuals in those crates in various degrees of decomp. Two males they identified through DNA. One is your missing bookie. The second is a Howard DelMonico, last known address, your neck of the woods."

Not exactly what I expected. I catch David's eye. "Thanks for calling, Detective Connolly. Won't waste any more of your time."

I hang up and signal for David to put us on speaker.

"Got some good news and some bad news for you, Duke," I say. "LAPD just called. The good news is they found Howard. Or what was left of him. In an abandoned warehouse in Los Angeles."

Duke inhales sharply. "What about the money?"

"That's the bad news. No mention of any money being found."

Duke slams his hand down with a crash that resonates through the phone lines. "Christ. Where did you say he was found?"

"In the office of a man we believe was his bookie. His body was discovered in the same place."

"Which," David chimes in, "might explain why there was

no money found. Whoever killed them probably took it."

"Our LAPD contact mentioned the bookie was on the bad side of some shady characters," I add.

Duke is quiet for a long moment. David finally asks, "What do you want us to do?"

Another four or five heartbeats of dead air. Then, "Trace his last steps. See if you can find out if he and that bookie were connected in anyway except the obvious. Then find out who he had gunning for him."

"Tall order," David says. "Might take some time."

"Take as long as you need," Duke snaps back. "I need some answers."

David catches my eye and shrugs. "Okay, Boss. We're on it."

David hangs up and we stare at each other over the tops of the computer monitors on the desk. We've had harder assignments, but not many.

"We're flying blind here," I mumble to David. "Doesn't Duke know any of his nephew's friends? He must have known something about the man before he was hired."

"He says not. He took him on as a favor to his aunt, who has since died."

"Any other relatives?"

David shakes his head.

I push myself back from the desk and stand up. "Listen. I have something I have to clean up before I can devote full time to this," I say. "Let me have the afternoon. If I get back before dark, I'll come right to the office. If not, I'll be in early tomorrow."

If I think David is going to argue with me about leaving, I'm wrong. "I can use some time, too," he says. "Before I go, I'll call Connolly back and see if he'll fax what he has on Howard's bookie. Maybe they had mutual friends."

I start for the door. "Or enemies."

TEN

I TRY TO REMEMBER THE LAST TIME I'D BEEN TO
Beso de la Muerte. I honestly can't. I know it was before I
married Frey and my mother passed away, but those months
are a blur.

Still, I make the drive almost by rote. It's too early for the
border crossing to be busy and I'm waved through. The route
to Beso de la Muerte isn't marked on any map. Most of it is a
dirt road wandering through clumps of cactus and scrub oak.
Even if you were tempted to give the unremarkable route a try,
you wouldn't get far. A magical barrier that protects the place
opens only for those Culebra allows in. Anyone else faces a
foreboding landscape and an overwhelming feeling of dread
designed to make the most intrepid of four-wheelers hang a
quick U-turn.

Once past the barrier, a familiar arroyo greets me on the
right, a lone pine on the left. This is the turn-off. Soon, Beso
de la Muerte comes into view, a rickety collection of dilap-
idated buildings with corrugated tin roofs. Only the saloon

shows any signs of life— Corrido music spilling out of an old-fashioned swinging door that hangs drunkenly from hinges twisted with time.

There are a couple of cars parked in front. Unusual for this early in the day. Most of Culebra's patrons prefer to come after dark. I park and glance around. Now that I'm here, I'm doubting what I'm about to ask Culebra. Janet Carlysle is certainly not his problem. I won't blame him if he sends me packing.

I open the car door and step out.

Culebra was the closest thing I ever had to a mentor when I was adjusting to becoming vampire. He helped me in more ways than I can count. I feel guilty that I haven't seen him in a long time. Even worse, I haven't thought about his ward either, a young Mexican girl we saved from some Narcos over a year ago. I don't even have a gift to bring her.

Guilt doesn't suit you, Anna.

Culebra's voice in my head makes me jump, then smile. Taking a deep breath, I push through the swinging door.

Culebra is behind the bar. He's grinning, a cigar clamped firmly between his teeth.

He looks exactly as I remembered—a long, lean drink of water with a Clint Eastwood squint and more lines on his face than a road map. He comes from behind the bar and holds out his arms.

All the hesitation I had about coming melts away with that hug.

"So," Culebra breaks away first and motions me toward the bar, "to what do I owe this unexpected visit? I can see just looking at you that you don't need a host. Marriage obviously agrees with you."

I take a seat on a bar stool and accept the Dos Equis Culebra holds out to me.

"How are you? How is Adelita? I can't believe I haven't seen either of you in over a year."

He puts a hand on my arm. "You've been through a lot in that year. Losing Max. Then your mother." He quirks an eyebrow. "Marrying Frey. Becoming a stepmother. Lots of changes in your life."

"I wish you and Adelita had been able to attend the wedding."

Culebra swipes at the bar with a towel. "I know David told you the reason. Adelita was in a school production—her first. It was the only thing that could have kept me away from your celebration."

"You made the right decision," I say, nodding. "If I'd been here, I'd have gone to her play, too."

Culebra reaches behind him and takes a photo from the wall. "Her last school picture. Isn't she beautiful?"

The curtain separating the bar from the back room parts. A woman comes through. She's human and, from the rapturous look on her face and the unmistakable funk of sex and blood emanating from her, I recognize her as a host. She nods to Culebra and me, then heads for the door.

She's followed by a male vampire. He's unfamiliar to me, but when he glances my way, his step falters. I don't know what vibe I give off, but it's always the same. Vampires sense

who I am and react with wary deference. I take another swig
of my beer and turn away. His retreating footsteps beat a quick
path to the door.

Culebra is grinning again. "It's probably a good thing
you're not a regular anymore, he says. "You would be bad for
business. Which brings me to the reason for your visit. What
do you want?"

No beating around the bush. I blow out a breath and tell
him about Janet Carlysle.

He listens, his face giving nothing away. When I've finished, he says, "You really think this is a good idea? To have
her live here while she's going through the change?"

"No. Not while…before. I want her to live here and see
firsthand what it means to be a vampire."

He laughs. "You saw the woman who just left. Did she
look like she suffered from the act? If anything, this Carlysle
woman would think she's doing humans a favor by feeding
from them."

"That's not the only way it happens. When a vampire loses
control, all kinds of hell breaks loose. You know you've had
to clean up after a feeding gone wrong. My idea is to let her
be a host for a while. Maybe get a taste of a not-so-sociable
vampire. I don't want her killed, you understand, just given
a better appreciation of what kind of club she wants to join."

Culebra hesitates. I don't blame him.

"I shouldn't have asked you to do this," I say, standing up.
"Chael tells me I'm crazy not to put this woman out of her
misery. I thought maybe—"

"Typical Chael," Culebra says. "Your plan might work. I can show her a side to the undead life not romanticized in books. What if it doesn't dissuade her? Or if it does, and she writes about what she's seen, what happens?"

I shrug. "I can't answer that. I wish I could."

I wait for Culebra to tell me I need to come up with a contingency plan and to take the situation more seriously. Instead, he shakes his head resignedly.

"Well," he comes out from behind the bar, "we'll give it a shot. When do you want to bring her down? Adelita is on a school trip to Washington DC and won't be back until the end of the week. This might be the right time."

He walks me to the door and we hug once more.

"I'll call Janet tonight. She's anxious to get started on this new *adventure*. Her word. David and I are going to be tied up with a job so I may let Chael bring her. I know you haven't met him yet. He's a piece of work but nothing you can't handle."

Culebra snorts. "If he tries anything, I'll shapeshift and bite his ass."

Culebra is Spanish for snake. I laugh. "That I'd love to see!"

When I get back to San Diego and drive by the office, it's dark and David's car is gone. I don't stop. I have some preparations to make. At home, I pour a glass of wine and head upstairs.

Janet answers on the first ring. "Here's what you're going

to do," I tell her without preamble. "Be here tomorrow at ten. Bring clothes for a week. Chael will take you to Mexico, so have your passport with you, too."

"Passport? Why are we going to Mexico? Why is Chael taking me and not you?"

"I didn't say you could ask questions," I snap. "So shut up and listen. You're going to learn firsthand what it means to be a vampire. You're going to do everything you're told. You'll be used as a host. If you want to become a blood sucker, you're going to experience what it feels like to be a blood bag. Maybe when you understand what drinking from a human host does to you, we'll talk about the next step."

Janet is quiet for a long moment. "You won't be with me."

"No. I have a life. I'm not going to babysit you."

"I don't trust Chael."

"That's your problem."

Another long pause. "Okay."

I cut the call. Dial Chael.

"You want me to take her to Beso de la Muerte?"

"I can't."

"You trust me with her?"

"I trust you'll do what I ask. She's afraid of you. Show her she has a right to be."

I can practically hear Chael grinning on the other end.

"Don't get carried away. I told Culebra the same thing. If she gets roughed up a little, that's okay."

This time Chael actually chuckles. "I may just need to feed myself."

"No." My voice is sharp. "You stick around and see no one gets carried away."

"You never let me have any fun."

"I mean it, Chael." I let the threat hang in the air between us.

He sighs. "I understand. See you tomorrow."

"No," I reply. "You won't. I'll be gone by the time Janet gets here. You just be here by ten to meet her. I'll be in contact with you. You know how to get to Beso de la Muerte?"

"I'll find it, don't worry."

"Fine. We'll talk soon."

I disconnect, sink down on the bed and close my eyes.

Well, I've set things in motion. I just hope I haven't made a mistake by trusting Chael with Janet.

Or vice versa.

ÆLEVEN

DAY SIX

I DRAIN MY GLASS AND DECIDE MORE WINE IS in order. The bottle is almost empty and I finish it off. I seem to be enjoying it more lately. Too much going on that I have no control over. Janet. Duke's crazy hunt.

Things don't get much better when I call Frey. John-John's grandmother isn't recovering as quickly as anyone hoped. She's still in ICU. I hear the frustration in Frey's voice as he tells me he doesn't know when they'll be back to San Diego.

I try to sound cheerful. "I understand. David and I are doing a special job for Duke. I may need to go out of town, too."

"Want to tell me about it? Is it going to be dangerous?"

I sigh. "No. It's a trace. A lost relative." I leave it at that. No sense in complicating matters by telling him that the relative was murdered.

"Duke's paying you to find a lost relative? Why? No. Don't

tell me. Has to be money involved, right?"

I laugh. "Of course. I'll call you every night. If John-John's grandmother gets better and you two can come home, I'll be back in a flash."

We chat for a few minutes and hang up. My phone chimes again almost immediately. Duke's face and office number pops up on the screen.

"Duke? What's up?"

There's a long pause. "Is this Anna Strong?"

An unfamiliar voice.

"Yes. Who's this?"

"You don't know me. I'm a friend of Duke's. He wants me to give you a message. You can stop looking for his nephew."

My shoulders start to bunch. "Why isn't Duke telling me this?"

A pause the length of a heartbeat this time. "Duke can't talk right now. He says you and your partner can take the day off tomorrow. Don't bother trying to reach him for a day or two. He'll be in touch with you when he's ready."

The call drops. I glance at my watch. Almost ten.

I've got my car keys in my hand and David on the line in the time it takes to get out to the garage. His cell rings through to voicemail. "David. Meet me at Duke's. Something's wrong. He's in trouble."

Duke's office is on Broadway in downtown San Diego, across from the Federal building. I pull into the parking garage and head to the lobby. There's a security guard behind a desk but his presence is more for show than protection. The twelve story building houses about two hundred offices for small businesses and law firms catering to the clientele of nearby city and federal lockups; the ground floor is a restaurant, a convenience store and a coffee shop. The coffee shop is closed but the restaurant looks to be doing good business.

The security guard nods a greeting.

I pause by the desk. "Seen Duke today?" I ask.

"Not since I came on duty about an hour ago. Want me to call and see if he's in?"

I shake my head. "No. I'll just go up."

Duke is on the eighth floor. The hallway is empty. When I listen, I don't detect voices or movement inside any of the offices on the floor. Outside Duke's office, I press my ear against the door. Vampire hearing would enable me to pick up the softest conversation inside, but I hear nothing. The smell of fresh-spilled blood oozes like smoke from under the door. The watery queasiness in my stomach hardens into ice.

I try the knob. The door is locked. No great obstacle for me. I put my shoulder against it and shove. The wood splinters around the lock and I'm propelled into the room. The small reception area in front is empty. Duke's office door is open.

"Duke?" I realize how stupid it is to speak. If anyone's inside, the door exploding would have brought them running.

My vampire springs into alert. I cross the reception area, hoping the smell of blood isn't Duke's.

It isn't. Duke is sitting at his desk, staring at a body

stretched on the floor at his feet. He looks up at me, eyes glazed, expressionless. In his hand, a knife, dripping blood.

I stoop to examine the body, listen for a heartbeat. The blood smell is strong and it awakens the lust in me, but the blood is no longer pooling. The man is dead. He's lying face down. From what I can see, he's a white male in his thirties, dark hair.

The Duke I know, usually boisterous and irreverent, is a ghost. His pale, sharp-featured face has gone slack, lips and eyes drawn down as if the muscles in his face dissolved.

"Duke." I shake his shoulders, trying to break through to him. Shock has rendered him deaf and dumb. His eyes are on mine, but lifeless.

Shit. I grab a tissue from his desk and pry the knife out of his hands. I lay it on the window sill out of reach. I take Duke's face in my hands and lean close. "Duke, listen to me. What happened here? Were you attacked? Are you hurt?"

He shifts in his chair, recognizing my voice. His eyes clear and he pulls out of my grip.

"Anna. What are you doing here?"

I step back and gesture to the body.

Duke follows my gaze. "Christ." He passes a hand over his face. "Did I do that?"

I perch on the corner of his desk. "Looks like it. The knife was in your hand. Who is that?"

Duke is slow to respond. So slow, I figure I'd better spell out what we're facing. "I have to call the police. I found you with the knife in your hand. Do you want me to call your lawyer? Jesus, Duke. What do you want me to do?"

"What in holy hell is going on here?" says a sharp voice from the door.

Duke and I both jump.

David is at the door, a gun in his hand. He looks from the body on the floor to Duke and me.

I look at Duke. "You'd better tell us, and quick. If anyone on the floor heard me breaking in, the police may be on the way."

David holsters his gun. "You did that to the door?"

"Cheap wood," I say.

Duke stands, finally looking ready to rejoin the land of the living. He squares his shoulders and pulls on his suit jacket to straighten it. He crosses from behind the desk, careful to avoid tracking through the blood. He's not a tall man, barely comes to David's shoulders, but he meets his eyes. "You're not going to like this."

David's look of surprise must be mirrored by my own. "What does David have to do with this?" I ask.

Instead of answering, Duke points to the corpse. "That's Taylor Talbott," he says.

David's eyebrows shoot up. "The financial advisor?"

"Our financial advisor." Duke shakes his head. "I should have told you sooner. I thought if we found my nephew, I'd be able to track the money. Now that he's dead…"

Something sparks in David's eyes. "What did your nephew have to do with Talbott?"

"I think you've guessed." Duke lifts a shaky hand to

rake over his balding head. "He and Talbott were working together. I didn't have you tracking Howard because he stole from me. I had you tracking Howard because he and Talbott stole from us."

"How much?"

The tone of David's question makes it clear he understands the implication of what Duke said.

"All our money," Duke replies. "The entire eight million dollars."

TWELVE

I'VE NEVER SEEN DAVID SO STILL. "ALL OF IT?"

Duke nods. "Our entire portfolio, which, as it turns out, was invested in a Ponzi scheme."

David sinks into a chair. "How can that be? We got statements every month. We read the business plan. It was sound."

"The monthly statements were fake. And since we insisted on reinvesting our profits…"

"They never had to produce any of those profits."

I'm listening but we have a more pressing problem. I step between David and Duke. "I don't know what you two are talking about, but I do know we've got a body on the floor and a bloody knife with your prints on it, Duke. What happened?"

David interrupts before Duke can answer. "Anna's right. I'm surprised her Superwoman act busting down that door hasn't brought anybody running yet. We should get you out of here until we can sort it out."

Duke shakes his head. "No. I'll stay here and call the police. You two are the only chance I have to figure this thing out."

"Duke, who was with you besides Taylor?" I ask. "Or was it Taylor who called me and said you wanted us to stop looking for your nephew? He obviously didn't know Howard was dead."

"No. It wasn't Taylor who called you. I'd never seen the guy before, but he came in with Taylor. From the way he was acting I could tell Taylor was afraid of him."

"Did he kill him?"

"He must have. One minute I was talking to Taylor, and the next…" He rubs the back of his head. "I was out. When I came to, Taylor was dead on the floor and you were leaning over the desk. The knife was…"

"In your hand. Jesus, Duke. Can you tell us anything about the guy?"

"Only that he must have been in on it. He knew Howard's name and that he was related to me."

I look around the office. "Did he touch anything? Maybe we can get prints."

"From the knife?" Duke asks hopefully.

David's expression is grim. "If he was thorough enough to put it in your hand, it's a good bet he wiped his own prints off first."

"What did he look like?"

"Tall. 6'2", I'd guess. 225 pounds. Blonde hair, brown eyes. No distinguishing marks that I could see. Jesus, he looked *normal.*" He passes a hand over his face. "Listen. You two have to get out of here. I'll give you a ten minute head start before I call the police." Duke looks around the office. Several files have been pulled out of open drawers and scattered on the floor.

I follow his gaze. "What were they looking for?"

Duke picks up an empty folder. "A list of our investments, our contracts, and the bogus monthly statements." He turns back to the file cabinet and bends to open the bottom drawer. He takes out a folder. "At least I still have this."

"What is it?" I ask.

"Names of the other 'investors' Taylor roped into his scheme. I did some checking when we first got involved." He presses it into my hands. "Take it. It'll be an eye-opener. David and I weren't the only ones lured in by the low risk, high yield bullshit Taylor was selling. Maybe some of the others don't know what's happened yet. Maybe Taylor's killer thinks he's plugged a leak by getting rid of him and my nephew."

"And not you?"

"I don't know anything that could hurt them," Duke answers. "Even if I did, making me the fall guy for killing Taylor effectively takes me out of the game. No one's going to believe a word I say when I'm charged with killing the guy who roped me into this scheme."

Duke starts pacing. "Whoever is behind this is smart. I'll bet everyone on that list dealt with someone different."

I shoot David a look to signal we should get out of here. I know most businesses are closed for the day, and the other offices on the floor are empty, but I still can't believe no one heard the racket I made breaking in.

A siren sounds from somewhere up Broadway. We are close to the station, and if it's coming our way we don't have much time.

"Go," he says, pushing David toward the door. "Take the stairs."

David takes the folder from my hand. "We'll get to the bottom of this as quickly as we can," he says.

He heads for the door and I'm right behind.

"David?" Duke releases a breath. "I'm sorry I got you into this."

David pauses and looks back. "Yeah. Me too."

———◆●●◆———

I follow David in my car back toward the office. It's hard for me to imagine David taken in by a Ponzi scheme. As long as I've known him he's been an astute businessman, our partnership profitable. I've let him handle the managerial side because he has a head for figures and much better organizational skills than I. If left up to me, our electricity or phones would have been shut off long ago, not to mention taxes unfiled.

What happened? I've always felt people taken in by a Ponzi scheme were either greedy or naive. David is neither.

When we get back to the office, I question if I should ask David if his lost "investment" is really going to wipe him out. He made a bundle while he played professional football. He has a couple of real estate holdings in addition to his condo in the Gas Lamp District, one being a cabin in the nearby mountains that's as luxurious as it is remote. He lives well—he has to with Gloria as a girlfriend. Whether or not he has a lot of liquid assets, I have no idea.

We pull into the parking lot together. Before I have a chance to get out, he's at my window. "You go on home," he says. "There's nothing we can do tonight. I'll go over this list. See who I know. We'll start making contact tomorrow. By then, we'll know whether the police believe Duke's story.

"Are you sure there's nothing I can help you with?"

"Just be ready to travel. Maybe that jet of yours will come in handy."

"I'll tell the pilot to be on standby."

David walks toward the office. His shoulders aren't slumped and his head is high. I wonder if I'd be that calm if someone told me I'd lost everything.

Of course, as a vampire, I have plenty of time to recoup investments.

I dig my cell out of my purse. Might as well see how Janet is doing with Culebra. I dial the number and listen as it rings. When the phone is answered it's with an abrupt, "Anna. What did you get me into?"

Culebra's voice is sharp with frustration.

"Janet giving you trouble?" I ask quietly.

"Trouble? She's a nightmare. Chael didn't even come in when he dropped her off. He couldn't get away fast enough. Now I'm stuck with her and she's the biggest pain in the —"

He's cut off before he can finish. Another voice takes over.

"Anna? Is that you? You didn't tell me this place was out in the middle of fucking nowhere. It's a dive. This friend of yours showed me where to sleep—on the ground, in a cave. No way. This isn't what I signed on for. I want to go home, and I want you to come pick me up right now."

Her indignant tirade runs down. I find myself smiling, but I let her stew for a long minute before I speak.

"Let's get this straight," I say at last. "You said you'd do anything to become vampire. Have you come to your senses? I'll come get you right now if you're ready to drop this stupid fantasy of yours."

A sharp intake of breath. "You have to come up with something else. Your friend won't even let me around any vampires. He's got me in the back doing dishes like slave labor. How can I find out what being a vampire is about if I can't talk to them? I thought you said I'd be a host and experience feeding from a human perspective. All I've experienced is dishwater hands."

I can't help it. I laugh out loud.

"It's not funny."

I compose myself. "Listen. If Culebra hasn't let you be a host yet, there's a good reason. He's being cautious about who he exposes you to. Not all vampires exercise restraint when feeding, and they can smell an overeager host. You have to trust me on this, although part of me wants to let them have you. If there's an accident, you will have asked for it, right?"

She's quiet. "How long do I have to stay?"

"Until Culebra thinks you're ready to make an informed decision. Jesus, you haven't been there twenty-four hours."

She sighs. "Why did I choose you to make me a vampire? I

could have found a hungry one that didn't have such scruples."

"And you might be dead now. I don't mean vampire dead. I mean dead."

When she doesn't have an answer, I say, "Put Culebra back on."

I hear a muffled exchange as she hands the phone back to him. "Sorry about the trouble," I tell Culebra.

"You owe me for this," he replies. I hear him tell Janet to go back to the kitchen and her grumbling retort. "She's a handful."

"I take it's a rough crowd tonight."

"Down from Oakland. Vampire biker gang. Bad mix. They brought their own hosts, but I've had to step in. I don't intend to offer body disposal as one of my services. Luckily, they're on their way south and will be gone by morning. Just stopped by for a soft bed and hard liquor, but not the crowd for Janet."

"Thanks for looking out for her."

Culebra chuckles. "Not easy to keep her busy. She wants to fraternize with the patrons, and don't think they haven't noticed her. I'll breathe a lot easier when they've left."

There's the sound of glass breaking in the background.

"Shit." Culebra's voice muffles as if he placed his hand over the phone. I can pick up shouting. "Got to go," he says. "A fight broke out."

He's gone.

I close my eyes. Poor Culebra. What have I gotten him into?

THIRTEEN

DAY SEVEN

AS SOON AS I WAKE UP THE NEXT MORNING, I grab the newspaper. Call me old school. I still prefer my news in print. The front page has no mention of what happened in Duke's office, nor does the City Section.

Strange since there are stories of two other murders that took place overnight.

I take the paper with me into the kitchen and start the coffee maker.

As I wait, I go through the paper page by page.

Maybe I missed something.

I almost skip the sports section but a headline catches my eye: "Star Athletes Lose Millions."

My gut says *read this*.

My gut is right.

David beats me into the office. He's seated behind his side of the desk, newspaper opened to the same article I'm carrying.

I help myself to coffee and join him at our big desk. I spread open my copy of the article. "I don't see your name on this list."

He looks at me over the rim of his coffee cup. "That's because Duke and I invested as a partnership." He sets his cup down, picks up the article and points. "D & D, LLC."

The main focus of the article is on one Clayton Oswald (no picture), a financial advisor accused of cheating dozens of professional athletes out of over fifty million dollars. A charge he vehemently denies.

"You don't think Oswald showed up with Taylor last night, do you?"

David sniffs. "I doubt it. He's under investigation according to the article. No charges have been filed yet. He'd be crazy to get mixed up in a murder."

"How do you think Howard and Sullivan connected with Taylor?"

David shrugs. "We'll have to figure it out."

I peruse the article. "I don't understand how this Ponzi scheme worked. It has something to do with selling tickets for sporting events?"

"That's the big picture," David answers. "Duke and I invested with Taylor a simple stock transaction in a company that allows fans to buy options to post-season sporting events. If their team qualifies, they purchase tickets at face value rather than pay scalper prices. It seemed safe enough. Fans loved it. Sports authorities loved it. From college games to the Super Bowl, fans snapped up the company's inventory."

"If it was so popular, how could it fail?"

David shrugs. "Not enough inventory? Insufficient marketing? Embezzlement? Who knows? When the company started to go under, Oswald siphoned money from other accounts he controlled to pump it up. By the time the company went into receivership, debt exceeded over seventy million dollars. While Duke and I thought we were building a nice little nest egg, our money was long gone."

I study David as he talks. Like last night, he seems passive. I remember something. "What about that file Duke gave you? Who's on it?"

David opens the middle drawer on the desk, withdraws a sheet of paper from a file folder, and hands it to me. "See for yourself."

The list is a "who's-who" of professional athletes from basketball to soccer, with well-known baseball and football players. At least fifty names run in two columns the length of the page.

I look at David. "Wow. This seems too big a deal to be relegated to the sports page."

"It's just the beginning," he says. "We'll be reading more as the scheme unravels."

He gets up and crosses the office to refill his coffee mug. I narrow my eyes at him. "You seem very calm for someone who just lost a bundle."

There's a long silence. His back is to me so I can't read his expression.

"David, what are you thinking?"

He turns. "I'm a dead man," he says.

I stare at him. "Are you serious?"

He nods. "Yep. I didn't invest my money. I invested Gloria's."

The snort that escapes involuntarily is half amusement, half incredulity. "Gloria's money? Are you kidding?"

He shakes his head.

I jab a finger at the newspaper. "How, for fuck's sake, are you going to explain this to her?"

He's back in his chair. "We'll cross that bridge when it comes." He shoots me a look. "I did some reading on Ponzi schemes. I know. Too little too late, but I think I know how they work. Oswald may be the one on the hook, but there's someone else behind him."

"How do you propose to keep Gloria dark until we find this mystery person?"

David allows a little smile to play at the corners of his mouth. "She's in Europe shooting a movie. Should be gone six weeks."

I shake my head. "How much of Gloria's money did you invest?"

"Bad news," he says. "Three mil."

This is the first time in our partnership I don't have a clue how to begin our search. We don't have a name. We don't have a picture. Our calls to Duke are unanswered. I don't know if that's a good or bad. I had many contacts in SDPD, vampire contacts, but they've all moved on.

Still, there's one resource left we haven't tapped.

"Maybe we should call Detective Connolly again," I suggest when an hour's gone by and neither of us have a workable plan. "See what their investigation turned up."

David reaches for his cell and scrolls his contacts. He puts the call on speaker and I lean forward as it rings.

"LAPD, Detective Connolly."

"Phil," David says. "This is David Ryan in San Diego. Anna's here, too. We wondered what you've uncovered in the Howard DelMonico case. There are a couple of loose ends we're trying to tie up."

We hear the sound of papers shuffling in the background before Phil answers. "Got the pathology report right here. Howard and the bookie were both killed about the same time. Coroner estimates they'd been dead two to three days. Different CODs, though. Howard DelMonico was dead before he was cut up. Since the torso and head are missing, can't be sure how he was killed. The bookie, Sullivan, however, was evidently alive when the killer went to work on him. He must have been after something. Whether or not Sullivan spilled before he bled to death, we may never know. As far as forensics, not much at the scene and what there was is still in the lab. We located a storage area where Sullivan moved his stuff when he closed his office. There were a lot of betting slips and a ledger or two, but nothing that pointed to a killer or a connection between the two victims other than the obvious."

"Think we might get a look at that storage area?" David asks.

"Don't see why not. It's been cleared as far as we're concerned. As for Howard's personal effects, we found bloody clothes and a wallet that was empty except for a driver's license."

"Was his ex-wife notified of his death?" I ask.

Again, we hear the rustling papers. "Ex-wife? We don't have any mention of an ex. What's the name?"

"Kitty DelMonico." I give him the address.

After a moment, he says, "When do you want to see the storage area?"

"How about this afternoon?" David replies.

"I'll leave the key with the desk sergeant. A uniform will take you out there. I don't think I have to tell you that if you find something we missed, it's your civic duty to hand it over."

He suddenly sounds very officious.

"No," David says smiling. "No, you don't."

FOURTEEN

THERE AREN'T MANY TIMES IN MY LIFE WHEN I
feel normal, but this is one. David and I kicking it old school,
a skip to trace, clues to ferret out. Almost like when we first
became partners.

There are obvious differences, though. We no longer go
to lunch or dinner the way we used to, or work out together
at the neighborhood gym. It's too hard for me to pretend to
eat, and too easy for me to forget that I shouldn't bench press
more weight than he can.

David has adjusted to the new dynamic. He thinks it's
because I have a husband now, even if Frey is absent more
than not. With Gloria back in David's life, that helps, too.
The fact that she's in Europe, however, may prove problematic.
It gives David a chance to recoup some of her losses, but it's
bad if he decides we should spend more time together since
Frey is also gone.

Tracey is due back in a week. She's always been a buffer.
She and David can do the things we used to. That is, if she's

accepted that he threw her over for his old flame.

These thoughts tumble through my head as I pretend to sleep. David is at the wheel, on the way to LAPD's Central Bureau headquarters. We'll pick up our uniformed escort and the key to Sullivan's storage locker. I hope we find something to point us in a direction—any direction—since now we have nothing to go on.

The key was waiting for us at the Duty Sergeant's desk, along with an eager young patrolman who drove us to the storage facility where Sullivan rented a locker.

The officer has the flush of a newly minted cop. He looks about twenty-five, clean shaven, carrying himself ramrod straight. His uniform is crisp, his shoes are polished, and his gun leather is conditioned to a high-gloss sheen. He shakes hands with each of us and directs us to his squad car, which is as spotless as his person. I wonder how long it will be before he relaxes enough to eat in the car. Probably not until a collar pukes in the back seat.

He asks how we managed to get access to a murder victim's effects, but David's answer is ambiguous enough to be plausible. There were insurance papers that somehow disappeared and Sullivan's widow authorized us to look for them. Since the locker was cleared by forensics and appeared to have no connection to his murder, there was no conflict.

The patrolman uses the key to open the padlocked door, then stands back so David and I can go inside.

The space is small, about 10 x 12. Boxes are piled against the back wall, a metal desk against the right, and a wooden file cabinet against the left. David approaches the cabinet first. It's locked. It's obvious the detectives got inside; none of the ledgers Phil mentioned, not even a betting slip, are in sight. They also must have taken the key since they didn't leave it for us.

I glance at the patrolman. He moved to stand beside the car. He's watching us, but not closely. Filing cabinets are notoriously easy to break into. David shifts to block his line of sight while I work on the filing cabinet with a lock pick. In minutes, the top drawer slides open. It's empty. So are the middle and third drawers. I slip my hand inside. It may be my imagination but the last drawer seems a tad shorter than the others. I press against the back of it.

Something gives.

David's eyebrows rise.

I let the false back fall. A key is taped to the inside. I pry it loose.

"Safe deposit box?" I whisper.

He gives a tiny nod. I slip the key into my pocket, shut the drawer, and relock the cabinet.

David and I move to the desk.

Like the cabinet, the drawers are empty. No false backs or bottoms here. The boxes are open containing clothes. After sifting through what looks like the contents of somebody's dirty hamper, we give up.

We rejoin the patrolman.

"Didn't find anything did you?" he asks, seeing us walk out empty-handed. "Our detectives are pretty thorough."

"I guess so," I answer ambivalently. Not thorough enough to completely pull open all the drawers of that file cabinet.

———◆●●◆———

Back in the car, I slide the key out of my pocket. "We have our work cut out for us."

David nods, knowing what I mean. There are no distinguishing marks on a safety deposit box key except for a number. 796. Seeing as there are thousands of banks in the Los Angeles area, assuming he used a Los Angeles bank, and millions in the country as a whole, finding a needle in a haystack would be an easier task than finding Sullivan's bank.

It's all we have.

I call Duke's cell. As we haven't heard from him since last night, I don't know what to expect. He could be in jail.

He picks up on the first ring. "Anything?"

The Tesla's Bluetooth makes that one word erupt like a bark.

"Not sure," I answer. "Where are you?"

"At your office," he says. "I've been waiting for you to get back."

"The police let you go?" David asks.

"The police never took me."

David and I exchange looks.

Duke heaves a sigh. "I left right after you and took the knife with me. Wasn't long before someone discovered the door had been blown apart." He pauses. "Anna, explain how the hell you smashed that door," but he doesn't wait for me, and forges ahead. "Anyway, the guy phoned in a burglary. Cops called me at home and I went down. The police don't know what to think. The dead guy was stabbed but no knife was found. Considering my line of work, they're leaning toward the disgruntled customer theory. For the moment, I'm in the clear."

For the moment.

David glances at his watch. "It's going to be a good two hours before we get back. Why don't you go home? Get some sleep. We'll call you tomorrow."

From the way Duke sucks in a breath, I know he's going to object.

"Not going home," he says shortly. "It's the first place the cops will come if they change their minds. I'm heading out of town. I know a place off the beaten path. I'm ditching this phone as soon as we hang up. I'll get a burner tomorrow and call you when I can."

Without waiting for a response, the call drops.

David starts the car and pulls onto the road.

I'm turning the key over in my hand. "What do we know about Sullivan?"

It's a rhetorical question since David and I both got our information from Connolly during that phone call this morning. I'm mulling over what the detective said when I realize there is one piece of information missing. "Do you think Sullivan was married?"

David shoots me a sideways glance. "Good question." He speaks Connolly's name, and the sound of a number dialing fills the car. The call rings several times then goes to voicemail. David leaves a message that we're interested in a contact number for Sullivan's next of kin, and ends the call.

I lean back in the seat, close my eyes. "Wake me when we get to the office."

"Next time," David grumbles, "you drive."

FIFTEEN

IT'S ONLY ABOUT 7:30 WHEN I GET BACK TO THE house. I debate calling Frey, but the prospect of learning there's still no change in his mother-in-law's condition is too depressing. I grab a jacket and head back on the road. I should check in on Culebra and our problem child to make sure he hasn't killed her yet.

———◆◆◆———

When I pull up to the bar, it's surprisingly quiet. That should be comforting, but there are only a couple of cars parked in front even though it's a Friday, so not comforting. Beso de la Muerte usually comes alive on the weekends.

When I push through the swinging doors, anxiety ratchets up another notch.

The place is empty.

Not even a bartender to greet me.

"Hello?"

My voice echoes in the stillness.

This is not good.

I make my way through the back and out to the path winding down to the "living areas," a little distance from the bar. This is Culebra's refuge for fugitives both human and not—a kind of sanctuary. Anyone can seek safe haven here as long as one rule is followed: do no harm. It's a rabbit warren of caves, strung with electric wire for light. I have no idea how far back the caves go or who might be in residence now. I pause at the opening to the main tunnel.

"Anyone here?"

My voice reverberates off the walls and ceilings like the toll of a lonely bell, finally fading into nothingness.

I pause. Should I go back to the bar?

A shuffling sound precedes a shadow approaching from the tunnels' rear. When the light hits his face, I relax taut muscles I didn't know tensed.

I recognize the figure. Thin, slump-shouldered, human. A doctor who has been here since my first visits to Beso. He's helped me twice—once when David was attacked by a vampire and once when Frey and Culebra were caught in a witch's spell. He kept them alive until I could save them.

I don't know his name. I've always referred to him as "doctor", even though technically he's not. He lost his license in the states because of a drug habit. From his haggard appearance, it's a drug habit he's yet to shake.

He approaches and a smile softens the crags on his face. "Anna Strong? What brings you here?"

He holds out a hand and I pump the dry fist. "I came

to see Culebra. The bar is wide open and empty. Where is everyone?"

He lifts his shoulders. "Seems everyone is off looking for a girl who disappeared."

My shoulders bunch. "Girl?"

"You know her, if I'm not mistaken," he says. "Brought her here, am I right?"

Jesus. I suck in a breath. "How did she disappear?"

"Just walked away. Culebra left her in the kitchen washing dishes, a chore she loathes, to hear her tell it. Next thing he knew, she was gone."

"How long?"

He purses his lips. "Thirty minutes? Maybe a little longer? Wasn't too busy tonight so Culebra pressed everyone into service. Can't figure out why they aren't back by now. She was walking. Couldn't have gone far."

I thank him and whirl around to the bar. I suspect Janet planned her escape well. Might have even had an accomplice, bribed with a boatload of money or, even worse, the promise to be a host.

No, that's not the worst.

The worst is if she's found someone who's agreed to turn her.

I could get into my car and retrace my route, on the off chance she's sticking to the road. She might have ducked out of sight when she saw me arrive. If she's on foot, though, she wouldn't make it past Culebra's invisible barrier.

Unless she's with another supernatural.

I made a huge mistake bringing her here, thinking I could change her mind. Chael had the right idea. I should have let him kill her.

I can't believe I'm thinking that.

I can't believe I want to kill her myself. She's been nothing but trouble.

I shake the thoughts away and climb into my car. I'm sure Culebra and his search party are scouring the desert in a fleet of ATV's.

I start the Jag.

Before I engage the gear, I pause.

A niggling suspicion.

If Culebra pressed everyone to look for Janet, why is the doctor still here?

Even if Culebra wanted the doctor to stay in case Janet came back, why isn't he in the bar?

I shake my head. It would be just like Janet to make a deal with the doctor—let her hide out until everyone was gone. Then he could sneak her out past the barrier and no one would be the wiser.

I switch off the ignition. There's a back way to the caves, one that winds around and comes out on top of the opening. Quietly, I make my way over uneven ground in vampire stealth. In less than a minute, I'm looking down at Janet and the doctor, making their way toward a clump of brush near the entrance.

While they pull apart the bramble, I send a message to Culebra:

She's here. Bring everyone back.

I get a torrent of invective in return.

I jump to the ground and approach Janet noiselessly. I grab her by the scruff of the neck, and she lets out a yelp.

The doctor whirls around. "We're in trouble, aren't we?"

Yes, they're in trouble.

Culebra left with the doctor for the caves. I don't know what punishment Culebra will dole out, but if it includes banishment, that's a death sentence. This has been the doctor's only home for years. I feel sorry for him and told Culebra Janet was likely behind the plan, but I don't know if it will make any difference.

Janet sits quietly in the back of the bar. The place is filling quickly. Evidently, Culebra closed the magical barrier to Beso after it was discovered Janet disappeared. Only I could get through—I'm sure Culebra wanted me to see what trouble Janet caused. The doctor couldn't have left either.

I'm sitting with Janet, who hasn't said a word. Unusual. Even more unusual, she looks mortified. Whether for herself or because she realizes the position she put the doctor in, I don't know.

When Culebra comes back and strides over to join us, she holds up a hand.

"I'm sorry," she says. "Please don't take it out on the doctor. He went along because I convinced him I was kidnapped and brought here." She shoots me a look. "Not exactly untrue."

My hackles rise, but before I can speak, Culebra leans toward her. "You are a stupid, careless, thoughtless young woman. When I heard what you did, my first impulse was to beat you senseless. I know Anna would never allow it. I'm going to ask you one question and how you answer it will determine if you stay or go."

Janet looks up at him, eyes round, mouth agape. "You'd let me stay?"

I'm as shocked as she. *You should have asked me if you could beat her,* I tell Culebra. *I might have surprised you.*

There's just the tiniest of quirks to the corner of his mouth. *Next time.*

Janet stares.

Culebra straightens and crosses his arms over his chest. "If you are still determined to become vampire, you will be a host for four days straight, starting this night. I will pick the vampires and you will do exactly as you are told. If you ask any of them to turn you before the four days, you will be brought back to LA and your memory wiped. I will personally see that your bank accounts are drained, your home destroyed and your career ruined. If you doubt I can, try me."

I don't know about Janet, but I believe him.

Evidently, so does she.

Janet nods.

"Say you understand and agree."

"I understand and agree."

"After you are turned, you will stay here for one month. You will learn how to feed safely. During that time, you will work at the bar. No whining. No complaining. If you pass that month, Anna will take you back to your home. She will also see that you come here to feed. If you miss one month, you will be executed."

I'm startled by that last statement. But Culebra's voice in my head says, *Go along with it.*

Janet's eyes are big, but she says, "I agree."

He turns to a vampire at the bar and motions him over. "This is Janet. She will be your host. It's her first time. No sex. Just feed."

The guy is a good looking twenty-something. Whether Culebra already spoke to him or whether my presence emphasizes the seriousness of what he is being told, he agrees.

Janet stands up.

I put my hand on her shoulder. "Are you sure this is what you want? If you're having second thoughts, this is your last chance to speak out."

She trembles under my touch but I believe it's from excitement, not fear. She leans close. "This is what should have happened as soon as I got here." She says quietly.

A thought springs unbidden into my head. Was this whole "running away" a ploy to make this happen? She's only been here one day.

I watch her follow the vampire into the feeding rooms in back.

Culebra takes the seat opposite me. "What's the matter?" he asks.

"We've been played," I reply. "She set this up thinking

you'd react the way you did."

Culebra's eyes go cold. "I suspected as much. Anna, I'm telling you, I won't be taken in again. If she steps out of line, just once, she's done."

I don't ask what he means by "done." I'm afraid I know.

———◆●◆———

I stay long enough to see the vampire leave Janet's bed and go back to check on her.

She's on her side, her hand pressed to her neck.

"Are you all right?" I ask.

She rolls over to face me and I see the answer shining in her eyes. "It was better than I imagined."

Culebra steps into the room. He tosses a set of sheets at her. "Change the bed," he says. "Then go help behind the bar."

The old Janet flashes and I think she's going to argue but the expression on Culebra's face stops her. She stifles a retort through pressed lips and smiles up at him. "Yes, sir."

Culebra and I exchange looks.

I shrug.

Should have let me beat her, he says.

SIXTEEN

DAY EIGHT

THE NEXT DAY, DAVID AGAIN MAKES IT INTO the office before me. Gloria being gone must make it easier for him to get out of bed in the morning. With Frey gone, it is for me.

He tells me he heard back from Detective Connolly and has an address for the wife of Howard's bookie. We don't waste any time seeking her out.

Sarah Sullivan isn't living like the wife of a bookie who was supposed to be as successful as her husband was rumored. The apartment building is not far from his office. It isn't run down, but the paint is chipping off the stucco. What is supposed to be a security gate hangs open on rusted hinges.

She answers the bell in a dressing gown, a cigarette dangling from her left hand, a coffee cup clutched in her right. She has bottle blonde hair drawn into a knot at the top of her head and pale blue eyes, accented heavily by black liner and mascara. The blush on her cheeks is the same shade as the red staining her lips giving her the look of an aging Kewpie doll.

She looks surprised to see us. Her mouth purses. "Oh."

Not who she was expecting, obviously.

David holds out his hand. "I'm Steve Jenkins. This is my partner, Olive Green. We're here from Security Life."

I almost snicker out loud at his choice of name for me, but the way she brightens up makes me swallow the response.

"Sarah Sullivan," she says, depositing the coffee cup on a table near the door in order to grasp David's hand. She pulls him into the room, barely glancing my way.

A common reaction I'm used to. Women are attracted to David like a compass needle to magnetic north. I follow them in, shoeing the door closed behind us.

She motions us toward a couch. When we're seated, Sarah places herself between David and me and asks, "Would you like coffee?"

Since the question is directed at David, I remain mute. He declines and launches into his shtick.

"First of all, Mrs. Sullivan," he says. "I want to say how sorry we are for your loss."

He pauses just long enough for Mrs. Sullivan to lower her eyes appreciatively. Then he continues.

"We represent the interest of Security Life. I have reason to believe your husband took out a life insurance policy prior to his death. I say 'reason to believe' because, although we have the preliminary paperwork, we are unable to find a signed copy of the policy itself. You have been named as beneficiary in the preparatory documents."

I've never understood the expression "ears perked up" before, but I swear that's exactly what happened.

"How much will I get?" she asks.

David holds up a hand. "I'm afraid I can't answer that until I have the policy. Do you have a copy of the policy by chance?"

Sarah Sullivan's face goes blank.

"Would you know where your husband would have likely placed such a document for safe keeping?"

No spark of recognition.

I chime in, asking bluntly, "Do you have a home safe or a safety deposit box in a bank?"

For the first time, she swivels to look at me. "I don't know," she replies slowly. "He didn't tell me much about his business."

The doorbell buzzes. She pushes herself to her feet and, with an officious toss of her head, she says, "Excuse me," and heads for the door.

She opens it to a man who steps inside and pulls her roughly to him, planting a kiss on her lips that would have lasted longer were it not for her pushing him away.

This must have been who she was expecting.

Awkwardly, she frees herself from his grasp and gestures to David and me.

"We have company."

The guy blinks and steps around her to check us out. He's got thinning hair and bad skin, and his suit hangs on his bony frame like cloth draped on a skeleton.

"You are…?" he asks.

Sarah plants herself in front of him. "This is Steve Jenkins and his partner…I don't remember her name. They're from a life insurance company. They say Harold took out a life insurance policy and I'm named as beneficiary." She's carefully enunciating each word, bestowing some special meaning to each.

He seems to get it. So do we.

He holds out his hand to David. "Pleased to meet you. I'm Donald Smith, a friend of the family. How much will Sarah get?"

A friend of the family? Right. David plays along. "That's the problem we seem to have. We know Mr. Sullivan inquired about a policy, know that his wife was named beneficiary, but there's been some kind of mix-up at the office. We can't find a finalized document and without that…" He lets his voice trail off despondently.

Donald turns to Sarah. "This won't do, will it?"

I take a turn. "Before you came in, I was asking Sarah if they had a safety deposit box. That would be the most likely place Mr. Sullivan would keep important papers. Don't you agree?"

Sarah frowns. "I don't know. Harold never told me about such things."

Donald takes her chin and turns her face up. "Think, baby. Maybe Harold has a safe here at home, or a locked drawer in his desk?"

Sarah looks disconsolate. I almost feel sorry for her. Donald's grip is tightening on her chin. I stand and step between them.

"You seem to know the family well," I say pleasantly. "Maybe you and I could go outside and brainstorm where we might find Harold's papers."

I'm smiling at him and, like David, I can turn on the charm, too. Donald doesn't hesitate a moment.

"Good idea. I have a few ideas we could discuss."

I'll bet he does. I take his arm and lead him outside. It's up to David now.

Donald and I stroll around the pool area. He's walking much too close, making sure his hip brushes mine with each step. Finally he says, "What was your name?"

"Olive."

He snickers. "You're not built like any Olive I've ever seen. You'd keep Popeye on shore, for sure."

I laugh enthusiastically. "How long have you known Sarah?" I ask.

He winks at me. "We've been friends for a long time, if you catch my drift. It's not serious between us. I'm a free agent."

He says it like it's the answer to my prayer. "Did you know her husband well?"

"Business associates," he says. "Helped out in his—" Suddenly, he stops himself. As dense as he is, saying something like he was a number runner for a bookie might not be the most prudent way to impress. "Anyway, we were practically partners."

"So you'd know where he did his banking, for instance?"

"Well, no. Harold held that part of the business pretty close to the vest."

"He must have paid you someway? Checks? Direct Deposit?"

"Strictly cash." That seemed to make him proud. "That way old Uncle Sam couldn't stick his nose in." Another wink. "Tell me. How much is Sarah going to get?"

I shake my head. "Sorry, I can't divulge that. If we don't find a policy…" I use David's tactics and let the sentence dangle.

He stops and turns toward me. "Come on. You can tell me." He puts an arm around my waist as if to pull me close.

I counter with a stiff arm that sends him reeling back.

He's tumbles into the pool.

When he comes sputtering up for air, I shrug apologetically. "Sorry. Lost my balance."

I don't think he believes me.

———◆●●———

Donald slumps away to change his clothes, telling me to let Sarah know he'll be back. I'm unsure whether I should go back to the apartment. If David is getting somewhere with Sarah, I don't want to intrude.

At the same time, I have Donald's message to deliver.

I start up the stairs and have my finger on the bell when the door opens.

David winks at me then turns to Sarah. "Thank you so

much for your help, Mrs. Sullivan."

She's beaming and I have no doubt he has good news to impart.

"Oh." I smile at her. "Donald says he'll be back later."

She looks confused.

"He had an accident," I say.

"An accident?" She's looking behind me in confusion.

"Got too close to the pool's edge. He fell in."

I can feel David's amusement. When he's composed, he turns to face her once more. "We'll be in touch."

SEVENTEEN

"ACCIDENT, HUH?" DAVID SAYS WHEN WE'RE ON the road.

"That guy is a creep. I need a shower." I sober. "But I have a feeling about him. He said he worked for Harold. Do you think he could be part of what got Harold killed?"

"Not really our problem," David replies. "I'll pass his name to Connolly. Let him check the guy out. Right now, we've got a post office box to check."

"Post office box?" I echo. "Not a safety deposit box?"

"Nope." David looks pleased with himself. "When we were going through Harold's papers, there was a receipt from the post office." He reaches into his pocket and pulls out a folded piece of paper. "Here."

I take the paper and unfold it, smoothing it against my leg. "He took it out just a month ago," I say, perusing the receipt. I shoot David a sideways look. "How did you get Sarah to turn it over? Didn't she want to check it out herself or at least accompany you?"

He lifts his eyebrows. "She didn't get a look at it. I managed to distract her long enough to squirrel it away."

"I feel sorry for her," I say. "You know Donald is going to browbeat her into looking for that 'policy.'"

"Which is why I took the receipt. If I'd left it, he might have found it and put two and two together the same way we did. I want first crack at that box."

I look more closely at the receipt. "The address is on Hollywood Boulevard. Should we check it out now?"

"We're here. Might as well." He glances at his watch. "It's after twelve on a Saturday afternoon. The windows will be closed but access to the PO boxes shouldn't be a problem. What's the address?"

He calls up the GPS and I speak the address. A map appears on the dashboard and a mechanical voice starts directions.

It takes us thirty minutes to make it to the post office from Sarah's apartment. There's metered parking in front but we still have to go around the block a half dozen times before a spot opens up. David parks and we climb out.

The post office is located in a beautiful old building that looks like it's from the late 1800s. There aren't many of these left. Most get bulldozed in the name of progress. We pass under the porticoed entrance into a rotunda with hallways that reach out like the spokes on a wheel. It takes a few minutes to locate a directory and to get our bearings before we start in search of the post office boxes.

There are literally a thousand of them. 796 is a box against a far wall. The biggest boxes are located here. This one is about a foot long and eight inches wide. David is about to open it when I stop him.

"Are you sure we should be doing this? Maybe we should give the key to Duke and let him see."

"We don't know how to get in touch with Duke," he reminds me. "If we did, it would take him hours to get here. Better to check it out and see what we're dealing with."

He slips the key into the lock. I'm holding my breath. The key turns, the lock disengages, and the door swings open.

The box is stuffed with sealed legal-sized manila envelopes. At first glance, they all seem to be addressed to Duke in care of this PO box. There are so many of them that a notice from the post office informing the box holder, Harry Sullivan, will have to bring the notice to a window to claim the rest in person.

I pull one of the envelopes free and tear it open. I tilt it so David can see.

Stacks of hundred dollar bills banded in currency straps of $10,000. I count ten in the envelope. I look up at David. "There's $100,000 in this envelope."

David whistles. "How many envelopes are there?"

I do a quick count. "Twenty," and shove the envelope back into the box. "What do we do now?"

He relocks the box and pockets the key. "Nothing," he says, "until we hear from Duke."

"This is more than the money Duke gave Howard," I say. "This may be money from the Ponzi scheme, which means Sullivan was involved. Donald must be, too. It's why he's hanging around Sarah. She's in danger, David. We've put her there. If he suspects we found something in Sullivan's things, there's no telling what he'll do to her."

I press my palms against my eyes. "We've got to get Sarah to a safe place until we can figure this out."

Suddenly the benign post office seems menacing and hostile. I know we're alone, but the uneasiness that we're being watched grows. There's one thing both post office boxes and safety deposit boxes have in common—they always have two keys.

I convince David to go back to Sarah's and pick her up. Take her to someplace safe. We hit a traffic snag on Holly-wood Boulevard and it takes almost an hour to get back to the apartment. He stays in the car and I run up the stairs.

The smell hits me before I get to the door. Vampire stirs and growls. It takes effort but I suppress the feeding instinct and stop outside her door. It's open. Just a crack, but enough for me to see the place was ransacked. Sarah is sprawled on the couch. Her throat is cut, blood saturating the cushions and rug.

I step back and look around. I can't see anyone looking out of a window or coming in from the parking lot, so I retrace my steps. If I stick around, I'll be caught up in another murder investigation.

David takes one look at my face and says, "What's wrong? Where's Sarah?"

"Drive."

He pulls out of the parking lot. "Where to?"

"Home. The farther away we are from here, the better."

He heads for the freeway. "What happened back there?"

"Sarah's dead. Think, David. When you were looking through Howard's papers, did you touch anything?"

David is silent for a moment. "I don't think so. I let her handle emptying the drawers. The only thing I touched was the receipt, and I've got that." He shakes his head. "Jesus, Anna. You were right. We should have never left her alone. If we suspected Howard hid the money, how hard would it be for someone else to come to the same conclusion?"

"Do you think they followed us, or just the same trail of breadcrumbs?"

"We've got to talk to Duke. Shit. He's supposed to call us today."

We lapse into silence—intensified by the noiseless car. It's like traveling in a space capsule. I'm afraid to voice that Duke may be next, except they already had him…whoever "they" are. Why was he allowed to live? Was he being set up as the fall guy? Why was I called and warned off? Whoever made that call surely knew I'd come—

"David!"

My voice is shrill, and David jumps in his seat. "For god's sake, Anna. You almost gave me a heart attack."

"Go back. Get off the freeway and go back to the

post office."

One thing I love about David is that he trusts my instincts. He pulls off at the next exit and in ten minutes, we're headed back into LA.

"Now what?"

"I've been so stupid," I say. "I should have figured it out when I was called to come to Duke's office. It's us. They're following us, and we led them right to the money."

EIGHTEEN

BY THE TIME WE MAKE IT BACK INTO LA, IT'S dusk and the Saturday date night ritual is in full swing. Hollywood Boulevard is bumper to bumper. My skin crawls with impatience. The only advantage we have is the key, and I'm counting that whoever is after us does not.

The devil on my shoulder whispers, *there are always two keys, remember*?

If we were followed because the second keyholder faced the same problem we did thinking it was a safety deposit box, we graciously solved that puzzle for them.

Shit. Shit. Shit.

"We led the killers right to the money." It's not a question. "We're being followed," says David.

"From the minute we showed up at Duke's office." I pass a hand over my face. "Duke is, too, I'm afraid."

"What now?"

"Get the money." If we're not too late. "It may be our only bargaining chip. We haven't heard from Duke all day, and that worries me."

"You think they got him?"

I turn my face toward the window. I'm willing to bet on it. He'd be safer if he was arrested.

We pull into a parking space and David goes to the rear of the car. He grabs a gym bag in the trunk that he empties. "We'll need something to carry the money in."

If it's still there.

The post office looks even spookier at night. The lighting is subdued, a nod to environmental consciousness I suppose, but its long shadows are not reassuring.

We're alone in the cavern that houses the PO boxes and walking on tip toes.

When David's phone trills, we jump.

It takes us a minute to compose ourselves. David grins. I try to calm my pounding heart.

He accepts the call. I can hear Frey's voice on the other. "It's your husband."

"Frey? Is everything all right?"

"You tell me."

I have only heard this tone once or twice. He's pissed. "Of course. Why would you think something is wrong?"

He blows an exasperated breath into the phone. "Your phone goes right to voicemail. You haven't called me in two days. I was getting worried."

I dig my phone out of my jacket pocket. I forgot to charge it. Has it really been two days since I called?

"I am so sorry," I say. "I forgot to charge my phone. David

and I are working Duke's case and it's gotten—complicated?"

"Is that another word for dangerous?"

He changes from aggravated to concerned.

"No. No. I'm really sorry. How is your mother-in-law?"

"Ex mother-in-law," he corrects, as if that's further proof I'm not telling him everything. "No change. I'm thinking of leaving John-John here and coming back to San Diego."

"When?" It doesn't come out the way I intend, not delightfully excited but awkwardly cautious.

"Is there a problem?"

"No." I slap my palm against my forehead. When I glance up at David, he's grinning at me. Damn it. "No. I want you to come home. When can you get here?"

"I'll make reservations for Tuesday or Wednesday. You sure you want me to come home?"

"Yes. I'm sure. I miss you."

"I miss you, too." His voice is soft again. "Charge that damned phone, will you? Call me tomorrow."

"I will. Give John-John a kiss."

I end the call and hand the phone back to David.

He's still grinning.

"Shut up."

At least the call served a purpose. It broke the tension we both felt since entering the post office. We no longer needed to sneak around. We were alone.

We can see to the farthest row of boxes where Howard's is located. David drops the bag to the floor and digs out the key.

The door swings open.

I sigh in relief.

The envelopes are still inside.

We stuff the gym bag with so many envelopes, we can't zip it closed. David takes the notice for the remainder and slips it into his jacket. "I'll have an ID made. I doubt the post office workers recognize one patron from another."

He shuts and relocks the door.

It hits me that if all the envelopes contain one hundred thousand, then we have at least two million dollars.

I move the .38 snubbie clip from the small of my back to the side. David does the same with his Glock.

We pause. David's car is parked right in front.

Sarah's "friend" Donald is leaning against the Tesla. He's looking away from the post office, casually smoking, as if waiting for a friend. When the cigarette burns down, he slowly and deliberately snubs it out on the hood of the car, then flicks the butt away.

David's breath catches. "Son-of-a-bitch."

He presses the bag into my hands. "Stay here. I'll try to get rid of him."

"Don't be stupid, David. If he's followed us, he knows I'm with you. He may not be alone."

David pulls the notice from the post office box out of a pocket and hands it to me along with the key. "See if there's another way out of here. Call Connolly and tell him I'm in trouble. I'll stall as long as I can."

"No phone, remember?"

"Shit." He makes a 9-1-1 call. "I'm at the post office on

Hollywood Boulevard. There's a carjacking going on right now. A Tesla. I think the guy has a gun."

He ends the call. "Go on. Get out of here, and take my phone. The Tesla has anti-theft security. He can't drive it away."

He pushes me back into the rotunda, but I have no intention of leaving. I watch from the shadows as he approaches Donald. Donald has a gun pointed at David's chest. He keeps looking back toward the entrance, asking where I am. I look around to hide the bag. As vampire, I could take care of Donald in short order, but I can't take a chance where David gets hurt.

There's an arched doorway marked "Restrooms." The doors are locked but take only some concentrated effort to get through. They bang open, but there's no time to consider whether anyone heard. There's another door inside marked "Custodian." I force that one, too, and shove the bag under a pile of mops and rags.

I race back to the entrance.

The Tesla is gone.

So is David.

I'm in a quandary.

How far can they get in the Tesla before the anti-theft device shuts everything down? What will Donald do when that happens?

I had to hide the money, but now I don't know which way they went.

The Tesla suddenly pulls up.

Followed by a cop car.

David gets out, produces identification, and tells the patrolman that after the car shut itself down, the would-be thief ran off down Hollywood Boulevard. He gives a description that is nowhere near Donald's appearance, and I just smile.

David has Donald in the trunk.

The patrolman, taking a second look at David's identification, breaks into a grin. He recognizes his name, asks for an autograph, shake his hands and they part like old friends.

NINETEEN

DAVID STRIDES BACK INTO THE POST OFFICE.

When he sees me, bag in hand, he smiles. "I figured you wouldn't leave."

"Donald?"

"In the trunk. The money?"

I gesture toward the restroom. "Be right back."

I retrace my steps, dig the bag out from under the pile of rags.

"Let's get out of here," David says.

In the car, David takes Donald's gun from a jacket pocket and slips it into the glove compartment.

I throw the bag into the back seat and jerk a thumb toward the trunk. "What did you do to him?"

"Not much. He drove us into an alley. We got out. He thought pointing a gun at me would make me spill what I took from Sarah. I told him we took nothing. He didn't believe me. I head-butted him, and he dropped like a stone. The rest was easy. Handcuffs in the glove compartment. Athletic tape from my gym bag. He's still out."

"Now what?" I ask. "Do you think he's the one who killed Sarah?"

"We'll have to find out. Where do we take him?"

"My house is out of the question, especially since Frey is returning. Your condo?"

He shakes his head. "Too public."

We're on the freeway headed south. "There is one place out of the way. Hasn't been lived in for a couple of years. There's a groundskeeper, but I can give him a week off. It's certainly private enough."

David glances over. "That place you inherited in La Jolla?"

I nod.

"You sure? You seem to have a lot of bad memories connected to there. Not that you've shared them."

I don't intend to. He doesn't remember, but he has bad memories there, too. "I've been thinking more and more about selling the place," I say. "We can see what kind of shape it's in. Kill two birds with one stone, so to speak."

There's a muffled thump from the rear of the car.

"Sounds like Donald is awake."

David frowns.

"Do you need directions? The house is on Mt. Soledad."

David touches the map app on the dash. "Just tell Tessie the address."

Tessie? I shake my head and speak an address I haven't thought of in years. I hold out my hand. "Let me have your cell. I'll call the groundskeeper. Tell him to take a vacation on me."

Skip Donovan is a flower child of the sixties—a little scatter-brained, but he knows gardening. He loved living on the grounds and, more often than not, slept outside under the stars in a sleeping bag instead of in the garage apartment I supplied him.

He answers on the first ring. It takes convincing for him to agree—evidently he's in the middle of planting spring bulbs. I sweeten the deal by offering a round trip on my jet to Victoria Island and the chance to see The Butchart Gardens. It's more than he can resist.

I call my pilot next and tell him to file a flight plan, and to wait for Skip to arrive. I also ask him to make arrangements for a hotel and give Skip traveling money.

I hang up. I feel David's eyes on me. "What?"

"Must be nice. Private jet. Unlimited funds."

I'm not sure how to respond. I paid a heavy price for those perks, a price I'm still paying in a way. Besides, I felt myself bristle, David has a nerve. "Like you aren't living the high life," I snort. "What'd you make as a professional football player?"

"I'm not being critical," he adds hastily. "I know how lucky I am. I wish you'd tell me the real story behind your inheritance."

He says it like he knows I've lied about the house, the jet, and the estate my family occupies in France. I have, but I doubt I'll ever be in a position to tell him why.

A long moment passes. The rest of the ride is spent in silence. The closer we get to the house, the tighter the knot in my stomach. I wish I could tell David how I hate going back to where I found him bound and gagged, nearly dead from blood loss. I wish I could explain how the vampire who pretended to be my mentor kidnapped him and fed me his blood. How it resulted in my taking a dying David to Beso where the same doctor who got mixed up with Janet showed me how to make him well.

A shudder passes. It still haunts me.

David remembers none of that, and I can't imagine telling him about it either.

Mt. Soledad is one of several exclusive places in upscale La Jolla, an enclave of the rich and famous. The place is at the end of a driveway that meanders about a half mile from the gated entrance to the front of a stone mansion. Skip had left the gate open. Once we drove through, I punched in the code to close it behind us. I doubt anyone will stumble upon the entrance and enter uninvited, but better not to take chances. Besides, there is a security service that patrols the neighborhood. They are aware no one lives on the premises except the groundskeeper. An open gate would invite suspicion.

David looks along the tree-lined avenue. He's wondering why I wouldn't want to live here. He'd understand if he knew what was done to him—done to both of us. All he sees are beautiful grounds and the silhouette of a multi-gabled mansion nestled among palm trees swaying in a gentle night breeze.

Almost magical.

Skip said he'd leave a key to the front door under the mat. Practical, but not original.

History has kept me away for years. Plenty of time to overcome the dread I feel, you'd think. My hand shakes as I fit the key in the lock. David hauls Donald out of the trunk. I'm relieved he's not beside me. I don't know how I'll react, taking that first step into a house I almost burnt to the ground.

I swing one half of the massive double doors open. My breath catches. I'm thrust back to the first night I came here, to a party, when the place was ablaze with lights. Now all is dark. Tonight, the floor-to-ceiling windows only reflect the night beyond like soulless eyes. There are drop cloths over the furniture and cheesecloth draped over the chandeliers.

I step inside.

Memories flood back. Why did I suggest we come here? The electricity has been off for years, and I don't know where to look for candles. The air is damp, smelling of mildew. I never asked Skip to air out the place, and now I wonder if, under those covers, there is furniture to salvage. Sea air makes quick work of fabric.

This was a mistake. I turn to tell David we have to find another place.

He's behind me, pushing a bound and gagged Donald ahead of him.

Donald is wide-eyed as he looks around. David has the same expression.

David lets out a long, low whistle. "Wow. The doctor who

owned this place before must have been very successful. Is the electricity on?"

I shake my head. "No. Maybe this wasn't such a great idea. We need candles and I don't know where to begin looking—"

David moves past me further into the living room. "What's through those doors?" he asks, pointing to the right.

It's the library. He didn't wait for me to answer. He's back in a minute.

"There's a huge fireplace and it's still set for a fire. That'll give us some light."

He grabs Donald's arm, shoving him toward the door. I follow. He jostles him down onto a chair. A dust cloud rises around him. David frisks him, smiling triumphantly when he produces a cigarette lighter. He has a blaze going within a minute.

Shadows leap and dance against the walls. David crosses to a set of French doors and swings them open. A brisk gust of air washes the room and sends the flames darting higher. I remember the wide balcony outside those doors. It hovers over the Pacific many feet below. You can't see the ocean in the dark, but you can hear the waves.

David returns from outside and stands in front of Donald. "Game time." He reaches down and yanks the tape from Donald's mouth.

Donald retches and gulps air. "Where are we?" he manages to gasp.

"Doesn't matter," David says. "You're going to tell us if you killed Sarah Sullivan."

"Wasn't me. She was dead when I got there." He looks up at me and David. "I figured it was you two—came back to search the place again. I didn't buy that insurance scam. You don't look like any insurance investigators I've ever seen." He sniffs. "The way this bitch moves, no way she—"

Bitch? I don't let him finish. I pinch his cheeks between my fingers until he squeals. "Don't be rude."

David chuckles. "Better watch your mouth, Donald. Olive has a short fuse." He takes my shoulders and moves me gently aside. "Okay, let's start over. How long did you know Sarah? None of that 'old family friend' bullshit."

Donald shrugs. "Since her old man kicked it."

"Who pointed you in her direction?"

"Nobody. I was his client—figured there might be money by romancing the widow. Word was Howard hit it big. When he disappeared, I thought he'd taken the loot and skipped. Then he turned up dead. It was a gamble, but maybe he told Sarah something that would lead me to the money. I was about to give up—she didn't know anything about his business, let alone a big score. Then you two showed up talking insurance. Something was better than nothing."

David slaps the tape back on Donald's mouth and gestures for me to follow him. We go into the living room.

"Do you believe him?" I ask after we close the library doors behind us.

"He isn't bright enough to lie," David answers.

"What now?"

"I'll call Duke again," David says. "If he's only interested in the money, our work may be through here." He digs his cell from his jacket pocket and speed dials. He places the phone on speaker and we wait through six rings before the call goes to voicemail. It's the same generic message Duke always uses. David leaves a terse message to "call us."

"Why didn't you mention finding the money?" I ask.

He shakes his head. "I don't know what's going on with Duke. Maybe the guy who ambushed him is holding him at his house. I think we need to get over there."

"And Donald?"

"We'll drop him off downtown. If he had anything to do with Sarah's death, the cops will look for him."

TWENTY

WE UNTIE DONALD AND SHOVE HIM INTO THE back seat. Instead of looking relieved, he is pinched with fear. "What are you doing with me?"

"Nothing," David says. "We'll drop you off back at the post office."

"You believe me?" he asks, relief brightening his face.

"Believe that you didn't kill Sarah?" I reply. "Not really, but I imagine there's enough of your DNA in her apartment that you'll have your hands full convincing the police."

That brief relief dissolves into a frown. "You have to help me."

I climb into the passenger seat. "Can't help you with the police."

David grunts. "Nothing will help you with the police." He turns the Tesla down the driveway.

"Wait, wait." Donald's arms flail. "I swear I didn't kill her, but I think I know who did."

David takes his foot off the accelerator and lets the car

slow to a stop. We both turn to look back at Donald. "What do you mean?" David says.

"I heard something once in the bookie's office."

He drops his voice. I reach back and grab his shoulder. "What?"

"Ouch." He pulls away. "You've got some grip lady."

"Imagine if I grabbed you by the throat. What did you hear?"

Donald pushes back in his seat out of my reach. "Sullivan talked with a guy he called Howard and some other dude. Howard argued his boss was getting suspicious and they'd better cash in now and get out while they could. The other guy said he wasn't ready to pull the plug. He had another fish lined up—a big one—and too much money at stake to pull out. Sullivan wasn't happy but it was like he was afraid of the guy. Howard, too. Not much later I hear Sullivan and Howard are dead."

David and I exchange glances. I ask, "What were you doing while this happened? No one objected to you listening while they talked over their plans to steal money?"

Donald blanches. "They didn't know I was there."

I think back to the office layout. I can't remember anyplace a man could hide except that tunnel and the door to the alley.

Donald continues. "I was there delivering betting slips. When Sullivan saw who was at the door, he told me to get lost. I opened the tunnel behind the board. I knew where it led. It was a way to get in and out of the office without being seen. I didn't leave right away. I was curious so I stood behind the door and listened."

"If you were behind a door, how did you know who Sullivan was talking to?"

"The security camera over the door. Before Sullivan buzzed them in, I recognized Howard. He was a regular. I never saw the other two guys before. I could tell by Sullivan's expression he didn't like them showing up like that."

"What did the other guys look like?" I ask.

"You know how those security cameras' pictures are kind of grainy. One was an average looking guy. Howard was taller so I'd say 5'10". Dark hair. He kept his back turned to the door, like he knew where the camera was, so I never saw his face. The other was taller than Howard, wore a suit. Sullivan called him—" he pauses, eyes narrow. "Taylor. He called him Taylor."

"Did you hear anything?" David asks, frustration clear in his voice.

"No, but I think one of the guys did Howard and Sullivan."

I shake my head. "What makes you think that?"

"I saw him again."

"Where?"

"Outside Sarah's apartment two nights ago."

"If you never saw his face, how do you know it was the same guy?"

Donald shrugs. "He had the same coat on. One of those long, leather things. I think they're called dusters. Don't see many of them in LA nowadays."

I raise my eyebrows at David. That is the most informative information we've received to this point. "We need to get in touch with—" I glance back. Donald studies me, waiting. We should not give him more information. "You-know-who," I say.

He nods and continues down the driveway. Donald is quiet on the long ride back to Sarah's. As we approach the apartment, David slows the car and parks half a block away. There are a half dozen cop cars in front. "You better get out of here," he tells Donald.

Donald doesn't wait. He scurries out of the car and down the sidewalk, disappearing into shrubbery without a backwards glance.

"No thank you for the ride." I cluck my tongue.

David stares down the street. "What now?"

"Find Duke?" I suggest.

David speaks Duke's name and the car dials Duke's number. After half a dozen rings, the call goes to voicemail. I leave another message and David disconnects.

We sit for a minute, watching the sky brighten. The charcoal of night dissolves at the sun's touch into fiery striations of red, pink, and gold. It would be beautiful if I didn't know the reason for the vivid colors—pollution. Even the sunrises in LA are fake.

David touches the ignition. "Let's go home. I need sleep."

I don't argue. As soon as he's back on the freeway to San Diego, my eyes grow heavy. I settle in the seat and fall fast asleep.

— ●●● —

"Anna! Wake up!"

David's shrill voice brings me out of deep sleep into consciousness. "What?"

It takes me a moment to process what I'm seeing as the alarm bells go off. We are blocked from the driveway of my house by five cop cars. Three cops are standing at the opened gate. Another cop comes from inside the yard. He's not alone. Frey is with him.

I barely wait for David to slow the car before I jump out.

Frey spies me and pushes past the cop accompanying him to rush to me. He hugs me so tight I push away a little before I can speak.

"What happened?"

Frey doesn't answer, as if he's not ready to release me from his gorilla grip. Finally, he does.

"Jesus Christ, Anna," he breathes. "Where have you been? When I got here and saw—" He breaks off, gesturing behind him toward the house. "The blood? I thought…"

"Blood?" David joins us.

Frey nods. "A lot of it. And the house," he squeezes my shoulders. "I'm sorry, Anna. The place was ransacked. I've never seen anything like it."

The cop who escorted Frey approaches now. He glances at a notebook in his hand. "You're Anna Strong? This is your place?"

I take Frey's hand. "It's our home, yes."

He's a trim looking thirty-something with a face lined beyond his years. I wonder what marked him like that.

His next words wipe those thoughts away.

"I'm afraid your husband is right. Whoever broke into your house was looking for something. The damage done took a great deal of time and was deliberate and methodical. I'm more concerned about the blood we found. Did you have someone staying with you?"

I shake my head. "No. My husband was out of town, and my partner and I were in Los Angeles all day. Are you sure the blood isn't from who broke in? Maybe he cut himself on something he broke or—"

The cop looks at me over his notepad. "He? Do you have a suspect in mind?"

I shake my head. "No. I'm assuming it might be someone David and I have turned over for skipping bail and since we've not had any women bond jumpers lately…"

The cop shrugs. "This doesn't feel like retaliation. This feels personal. There are blood spatters traceable from room to room, as if someone was dragged along and beaten systematically as the perpetrator worked his way through the house. My guess is that he or she was looking for something specific." His eyes grow cold. "Do you have any idea what that might be?"

David and I exchange glances. His barely perceptible nod tells me he's thinking the same thing I am. Whoever trashed my house was looking for the money we have in David's car.

TWENTY-ONE

DAY NINE

IT'S THREE HOURS BEFORE WE'RE ALLOWED back into the house. We're surrounded by police. David and I say nothing about the money or what we suspect. When we are finally allowed inside and see the destruction, I'm transported back to another time—when I came home to find my house on fire. While the walls are standing this time, there's as much devastation.

Frey keeps a tight hold on my hand as we go through room after room. Every piece of furniture was overturned, every cushion ripped open, and every bookcase tipped. All of the clothes in the closet are strewn over the floor. Even John-John's beloved race car bed was turned over. My breath catches in my throat—first with sorrow, then anger.

Frey feels the shudder that passes through me. "We can fix it," he says quietly.

I'm happy he's with me, but so is David, and it keeps me

from unleashing the rage only vampires could quell. I have to swallow it.

"Be glad John-John is not here," David says.

"I am, believe me." I look up at Frey. "You weren't supposed to come home until next week."

Frey smiles. "There was something in your voice when we talked that sounded off. I decided to come home sooner. John-John is well looked after. There are a lot of people on the reservation who love him."

I know and I'm grateful. I'm grateful that Frey is here.

I look around. "I guess we have to get a hotel room."

David waves a hand. "No need. I have an extra bedroom."

A thought hits like a thunderbolt. "My God, David. What if they trashed your place, too?"

We waste no time rushing back to David's car and head downtown. When we pull into the condo's garage, we're not met with the police like at my house. It's perfectly quiet.

We head up in the elevator.

Still nothing.

All the same, we approach the door cautiously. Frey and I stand to the side as David draws his gun and quietly slips his key into the lock. He pushes it open and we pause, waiting for—

"Empty."

I release my breath in a rush.

David holsters his gun and we follow him inside. He reaches beside the door and flips on the light. He makes a tour of the condo while Frey and I wait. When he returns, he's shakes his head.

"Maybe they haven't been here yet," I say.

"I have another explanation," David says. He's crossed to the bar and grabs a bottle of Glenmorangie Single Malt Scotch and three glasses. He motions us to take seats and settles onto the couch. He pours a good stiff two fingers into each glass and passes them to me and Frey. He adds, "I don't think we are being followed. I think Duke was hiding in your house."

The scotch smells like butter and tastes like pear and lemon. It's a momentary distraction from David. When the first sip settles and my head clears, I look up. "Why would you think that? Jesus. You think the blood was Duke's?"

He nods.

"How would he get into the house?" Frey asks.

"He has a key," David answers. "He has a key to both our places."

"He does." I'm on my feet, pacing. "In case we needed him to retrieve something for us while on the road."

"If it's Duke's blood, the police will know once they run DNA. It's on record, as is mine and Anna's."

Thankfully, before I became vampire, I think. I'm not sure what my blood would show now.

"There was a lot of blood," Frey says quietly.

"Too much," David adds.

"It's time you tell me what you're working on," Frey says.

———◆●●◆———

By the time we've filled Frey in, it's almost noon. None of

us have slept and since we can't think of anything else to do, David makes up the guest room bed for us and we retire. I strip my clothes off and climb naked beside an equally naked Frey. For the first time ever, sex isn't something either of us are interested in. I fall asleep before he does.

I awake to the smell of bacon. I roll over to find Frey has already woken up. The clock on the bedside table says 6:30. I gather my clothes, head for the guest bathroom, and take a quick shower. I hate having to redress in yesterday's clothes but don't have a choice. By the time I join the guys, Frey and David are seated at the breakfast bar, plates of eggs and bacon in front of them.

Frey gets up and pecks me on the cheek. "I told David you probably wouldn't be hungry." He crosses to the counter and pours me a cup of coffee.

I take it and sip.

David looks sideways at me. "She's never hungry. Don't know how she keeps going. Gloria thinks she has an eating disorder."

I almost spit coffee. I have the ultimate eating disorder.

Frey doesn't miss a beat. "I was worried, too," he says, "but it's her metabolism. Her doctor says she's healthy as a horse, and as long as she eats the right things and takes her vitamins, she'll be fine."

He squeezes my shoulders and resumes his place at the breakfast bar. I sit next to him.

"Enough about my metabolism," I grumble. "What the hell are we going to do about my house?" The moment I speak, I wince. "I can't believe I said that. David, we've got to track Duke down."

"If he's still alive."

Frey lays his fork on his plate. "We need to do something about that." He eyes the gym bag on the end of the counter.

"Tomorrow morning we'll put it into our safe in the office," David replies. "It's too much money to take to the bank without having to answer questions."

"I suggest we go to Duke's tonight," I say. "Maybe we'll find something that points us toward whoever has him."

"You have a way to get in?" Frey asks.

"Only years of picking locks," David answers.

———◆●◆———

Duke lives in a city south of San Diego, Chula Vista. You wouldn't expect a successful bail bondsman to live in this type of neighborhood. It's an average, middle-class, cookie cutter, family street complete with picket fences and mini-vans in the driveways. His house is a two-story stucco box with climbing roses on either side of a gated driveway.

We park on the next block and walk over in case whoever took Duke brought him back to his home. The house is dark. The neighborhood is quiet, creepy. It's a change from the bustle of the beach community where I live, or the lights and noise of David's block downtown.

A few people are taking evening walks, some pushing strollers, some with dogs on leashes, but they nod and smile and generally pay us no attention when we stroll into Duke's driveway, and make our way to the back. Duke may not be acquainted with many of his neighbors but they, on the other hand, appreciate a quiet, single man who keeps to himself and maintains a well-manicured yard.

The back yard is the same as the front: neat, grassy, a flowerbed along the rear fence. David works on the door. We are aware Duke must have wired the place with an alarm, but we'll cross that bridge once we're in. It takes David less than five minutes before the tumblers fall and the door opens. We pause, waiting for indication that we've tripped an alarm.

Nothing.

We venture further inside and look for the alarm panel. We find it in the front hall. It's not set.

Duke must have either been taken, or he left in such a hurry, he neglected to set it.

David flips on a light in the living room. It doesn't look disturbed. Puzzling, since it makes sense whoever was looking for money would start here.

"I don't get it," David says, indicating the same thoughts.

We go from room to room. No open drawers, no strewn clothes. Not even a chair pulled out from the dining room table. Duke's taste runs to spare, modern neutral tones—and the only decorative items are a couple of pictures on a console. I pick one up. The couple are in their twenties, standing arm in arm against a backdrop of the Belmont Park coaster.

I show the picture to David, who shrugs. "Have no idea," he says.

I don't either. Duke never spoke of family, and I'm

ashamed I never asked. I replace the picture, hoping our next job won't be tracing Duke's next of kin.

"We're back to square one," I announce to no one in particular.

"Not exactly," David says. "We found the money."

The front doorbell chimes and we jump.

"Should we answer?" David whispers.

"May as well," I reply, heading for the door. "We aren't doing much good just standing here."

I look through the peep hole. A Mr. Roger's look-alike is smiling as if knowing I'm staring at him. He's tall, thin, dark hair peppered with gray, wearing a cardigan sweater complete with white shirt and knotted tie.

I pull open the door.

"You must be Anna," he says, taking a step inside.

Startled, I take a reflexive step back.

He holds out a hand, "I'm Steven Peters. Live next door. Norman said to expect you, and here you are."

Norman? In all the years David and I worked for Duke, I never knew his first name. It's clear why he'd want to be known as *Duke* professionally.

Mr. Peters looks over my shoulder.

"You must be David. Norman described both of you perfectly. You, sir," he eyes Frey, "I don't believe he mentioned you."

Frey steps forward. "Friend of a friend."

Mr. Peters accepts his hand.

"You said Du—Norman—said to expect us."

Mr. Peters turns toward me. "Yes. Day before yesterday. He came to see me. Seemed nervous. Said he had to leave town for a while but had a message for you and David. I asked why he didn't deliver it himself. It was too important to leave on an answering device. He knew you'd be coming by and said to watch for you."

He straightens his tie. "I said I would. Norman has done me favors many times. I was happy to return this one."

I shift from one foot to the other with impatience. "The message?"

"It's a post office box. Number 796."

I practically wilt with frustration. "That's it?"

I can't keep the disappointment from my voice.

Mr. Peters looks at me with a mixture of his own disappointment and irritation. "What were you expecting?"

David steps between us. "That's the entire message? There isn't anything else?"

"No. That is it. Your reaction is puzzling. Norman thought he passed on some very important information. Obviously, he is mistaken."

It was important information a day ago. I wonder how he figured out we had the key?

"Thank you, Mr. Peters." David takes the guy by the elbow and ushers him toward the door. "We appreciate your giving us Norman's message. We'll lock up here and be on our way."

"Before you go," I say on a whim, "have you seen anyone hanging around the neighborhood? Any strangers? I imagine a nice, quiet neighborhood like this has an active Neighborhood

Watch program."

That brings a smile to his face. "We do. Yes. A day ago there was a stranger. I noticed him because he wore a long coat during a seventy-five degree day. He walked back and forth in front of Norman's house. I was about to confront him when he left. Got into a car and drove off."

"You wouldn't have a license plate number, would you?"

The smile widens. "Better than that. I have video."

TWENTY-TWO

I FIGHT AN OVERWHELMING URGE TO THROW my arms around Mr. Peters. A video! We can finally get a look at this elusive "duster man" we're chasing. If we're really lucky, a license plate to pin a name on him!

Frey and I run Mr. Peters out of Duke's house. David stays behind to lock up but he's soon with us, ushering into a chintz and tchotchke living room worthy of an English revival country house. Flower curtains, flower upholstery on the chairs and couch, every inch of table/shelf space full with vases, figurines, and porcelain figures. I wonder what Duke, with his simple Spartan tastes, thought the first time he came here.

Mr. Peters walks over to a desk and returns with a laptop. He motions us to take seats around a coffee table. He opens the laptop, taps on the keyboard, then turns the screen to us.

"This view is from the camera mounted on my front porch. It's motion activated."

I'm puzzled by the system's sophistication. The camera is mounted on the roof. It sweeps back and forth a couple of times, reacting to cars passing by on the road. The view encompasses the front of the houses on either side of Mr. Peters and the three across the street.

"This is a pretty elaborate system," I remark, "and this neighborhood, pretty quiet and cohesive. What made you install it?"

Mr. Peters smiles. "Norman's idea. He paid for the whole thing. Wanted our little block secure."

Wanted his house secure, more like. While we don't see a safe inside, I bet he has one. I'm tempted to ask Mr. Peters what his neighbor does for a living, but I decide against it.

The camera continues its sweeps but slows and zooms in on a car stopping in front of Duke's house.

Frey, David, and I lean in.

The guy who climbs out of the car is dressed in all black—jeans, tee-shirt, and that long leather coat. He has a wide-brimmed hat that successfully hides his face from the camera. His outfit couldn't be more conspicuous, but the way he strides purposefully toward Duke's front door, he obviously doesn't care. We can't see him on the porch, but he's back on the sidewalk a few minutes later. He looks up and down the block, allowing a peek at his face for the first time.

"Can you zoom in on his face?" I ask.

Mr. Peters pauses the video and touches a few more keys. The camera refocuses and, though it's grainy, we have our first look at duster man.

I don't recognize him. He's got an angular face, blue or green eyes, a straight nose, and pointed chin.

"Could you print that?" David asks.

A printer whirs into life. Mr. Peters looks particularly smug as he hands David the photo.

"Great system," I say. "What about the car?"

Again, Mr. Peters is busy at the keyboard. He fast-forwards through the guy pacing in front of Duke's home. He gives up and gets back into a light sedan. When he pulls away, Mr. Peters pauses the video again, zooms in, and takes a screenshot. The picture he hands us this time is of the sedan with California plates, which we can clearly read.

David and I exchange satisfied looks.

"This is going to help a lot," I say, standing up.

For the first time, Mr. Peters looks concerned. "Can you tell me what's happening? Is Norman in trouble? What can I do to help?"

David pulls a business card from his pocket. "Keep doing what you're doing. If he shows up again, call me on my cell. Don't approach him. We don't think he's hurt Norman, but we suspect he's hurt others. He's dangerous. Norman wouldn't want you to get hurt."

Mr. Peters ushers us out more somberly than he showed us in. We assure him he's been an immense help and a good friend, and we will keep him informed. We ask him to keep this to himself. He agrees.

When he shuts the door behind us, I turn to David. "Let's get to the office and run the plates."

Frey's cell phone chimes. He answers and listens, frowning, then holds the phone out to me. "It's for you."

His expression is guarded. He will not tell me who's calling for a reason. I take the phone but before I can say hello, Chael bellows at me.

"Jesus Christ, Anna. Don't you ever pick up your fucking messages? I left twenty since last night."

For someone who just started speaking English regularly, he picks up swearing quickly. I bite back a sarcastic retort because he's right. My phone's been dead since I forgot to charge it the day before yesterday. I move away from David and Frey.

"What is it?" I whisper.

"You need to get down here now."

"Down where?"

"Where do you think? Where you dumped that bitch, Janet."

"What did she do now?"

"You're not going to believe it. Just get down here."

He doesn't wait for me to answer; the call is dropped.

I hand Frey's phone back to him, and David looks at me with puzzlement. Frey knows where Janet is. David doesn't, for obvious reasons. I debate what I say to get away.

"I'll ride with you back to the office," I say finally. "Frey, help David track down that license plate. I'm going to leave you two for a while."

David looks as if I suddenly sprouted an extra head. "What's more important than finding Duke?"

Frey picks up without missing a beat. "Do the police want to talk about what happened at the house?" he asks.

Bless him, offering me a reasonable excuse to get away.

"They want to see me right away."

David's frown deepens as he glances at his watch. "It's almost nine o'clock. Kind of late, isn't it?"

I shrug. "Maybe they got a lead."

Frey steps up again. "You go. David and I will see what we can dig up."

It's a quick ride back to our office, where I left my car—when? Was it really only two days ago?

When I'm in my car, Frey leans in and pecks me on the cheek. "Come back as soon as you can," he says. "Be careful down there. I assume this is more about Janet."

I nod. "I made a huge mistake trying to reason with that woman. I don't know what she's up to now."

He turns to David, then turns back around. "Charge your damned phone."

I mock salute…and dig my phone out of my pocket and the charger out of the glove compartment.

———◆●●◆———

I've never seen so many cars parked in front of Culebra's bar. I have to park two blocks down and make my way up a rickety sidewalk. Upbeat Mariachi music charges the still night air with cheerful buoyancy I'd never expect from a bar for vampires and their hosts. Certainly, it was never a choice of Culebra's, who always prefers the shrill, storytelling Corrido ballad.

Pushing through a crowd of primarily hosts, I spy Culebra behind the bar. His back is to me, and he is talking to someone animatedly. Before I get closer, a hand reaches out and tugs me from behind.

"It's about time you get here." Chael is dancing with frustration. He waves a hand around. "Look at this place."

The bar has a different atmosphere than I expect. There are couples, even vampires, dancing to the music, who don't usually show much emotion among their own kind. They look—well—cheerful. The place was painted, the bar redone, and, I sniff, bar-b-cue? The doc comes from the back with a plate of ribs. The human contingent gathers around him enthusiastically.

I smile. "It's different," I say. "What's the big emergency? What did Janet do now?"

"What did she do?" Chael echoes shrilly. "This. She's done this."

"You can't be serious. You called me here because Culebra is having a party?"

Chael's face drops. "A party? It's like this every night."

He's coming here every night?

I take another look around. "Looks like everyone is having a good time. What's the problem?"

Before he can reply, a familiar voice calls to me.

"Aunt Anna! When did you get here?"

I turn to see my "niece" Adelita hurrying toward me. She flings her arms around me, and I bask in the warmth of her hug before stepping back to look at her. It was too long since I've seen the radiant teen standing before me. The pinched features of a child kidnapped by drug narcos and forced into sexual slavery are gone. Her smile is sunshine, her brown eyes spark with life. She's beautiful, and I'm overcome with emotion.

I pull her into another hug.

Adelita laughs. "I'm happy to see you."

My guilt bubbles to the surface. "I should have come sooner."

She waves a hand. "You're busy, and you have a son now! When do I get to meet him?"

She takes my arm and steers me toward the bar. Behind us, I hear Chael's irritation, *We aren't done.*

I don't answer.

Culebra doesn't see me until Adelita calls him.

I see who he is talking to.

Janet.

Both faces grin as I approach.

I can't believe my eyes.

Culebra has a tee on with a colorful skull and *Dia De Los Muerto*s printed under it. I've never seen him in anything other than faded long-sleeve shirts and occasionally a poncho, á la Clint Eastwood.

Janet is wearing an elaborately embroidered Mexican off-the-shoulders blouse and skirt. She has a rose in her hair. That surprises me more than anything else.

Adelita steps behind the bar to join them and Janet puts an arm around her shoulders. I expect Adelita to pull away. Instead, she leans forward and kisses Janet's cheek.

I teeter between astonishment and jealousy.

They look like a family.

A family.

Culebra reads my reaction, and my thoughts.

Surprises me, too.

I don't know how to react. Janet's been here four days and the three have suddenly bonded?

Culebra comes around the bar to my side. *Let's talk.*

My head spins as I follow him into the back. I expected to find the place in ruins after the way Chael demanded I come to the bar…torched, maybe, by Janet. Instead, there's music, dancing, and a room of vampires and hosts having fun.

I know what you're thinking. Culebra's voice is in my head.

Of course you do, I reply sarcastically. *You're reading my thoughts.*

He laughs. "That helps," he says aloud. He motions me to a chair and I sink into it. "I don't know how to explain. Janet isn't a witch, is she?"

His tone is playful, but his question gives me pause. Maybe she is a witch.

Once again, Culebra laughs. "No. I'm pretty sure she's not."

"How do you explain—" I gesture to the other room, "That."

He shrugs. "Damned if I know. One day I want to kill her, the next, Adelita comes home from her school trip and she and Janet form an instant bond. They put their heads together and livened the place up. They go on a shopping trip to San Diego and come back with paint, varnish, and a bar-b-cue.

A bar-b-cue! They decided the vamps and hosts should have fun…and it's working. Business has never been better. Hosts come here to spend and make money. Vampires no longer feed and run. They stick around to drink and dance. Next week, Janet plans to buy a pool table—"

"Hold it. A pool table?"

My head explodes.

"I know. Crazy."

Beyond crazy. "What about Janet's desire to become vampire? Has that changed?"

"She doesn't talk about it anymore. She no longer offers herself as host. I'm telling you, Anna. She's a different person."

I think I know why. "Because of Adelita?" I ask, but it's not really a question. It makes sense in a sweet, maddening way. "She has no family. No one. In Adelita, she sees a chance to become a big sister," I narrow my eyes at Culebra. "Or a mother."

Culebra doesn't argue, confirming it crossed his mind, too.

"Adelita obviously adores her. What if she changes her mind?" I ask quietly. "What would it do to Adelita if she were to leave?"

"I won't."

Janet crosses into the room. She looks up at Culebra. "Could I speak to Anna a minute?"

He glances my way and I nod. *It's a good idea.*

Janet waits until he's gone and closes the door. "You have no reason to believe what I'm about to say, but I hope you'll hear me out." She turns and squares herself up to me. "I was a train wreck when I arrived. I believed immortality was the only thing left in this world to satisfy me. I have more money than I need, no responsibilities, no dependents. I was lonely and bored. When I learned about the existence of vampires, it seemed I could finally be a part of something bigger than myself. It was a club, a family, I could join."

She sits across from me. "Here, I realize there is no vampire club. No vampire family. Every vamp that walks into that door walks in alone. You are the exception. It's because you don't let your human side wither. You cling to it.

"Here with Culebra and Adelita, I found something, too. I found a darling girl who never had a real mother, who speaks of you as the one who saved her, fought for her, when her own mother didn't. She sees Culebra as the angel who saved her from poverty and gave her the opportunity to go to school, to become something. I want to be a part of that. I have something to offer her, and Culebra." She laughs. "He's a character, you know? He acts gruff and scary, but he melts around Adelita. I'm not sure what he is. I know he's not completely human, nor is he vampire. He doesn't feed. He hasn't shared that part of himself with me yet, but when he trusts me, he will. I can wait."

She stops, and we sit quietly for a moment.

Conflicting emotions swirl around inside me. I can't sort them fast enough to reply. I want to believe her. Adelita needs a female role model she can relate to. If Janet is sincere...

"What happens if you get bored?" I ask. "If you decide you miss that big mansion in LA? Four days ago you yelled at me because you slept in a cave."

She grins. "We figured that out. Culebra is letting me build a cabin out back. Nothing fancy—a couple of bedrooms. One is for Adelita when she returns home from boarding school on the weekends and one is for us."

"Us?" The word squeaks out.

Her face reddens. "Well, we came to an understanding. I can't say we're in love, but I think that will come. He's not had anyone in his life for a long time. We're taking it slow—" The blush deepens. "Honestly, Anna, sex with him is—"

I hold up a hand. I don't need to hear anymore.

I stand up, look at her, and resort to the only way I know how to impress her with the sincerity of my words.

"If you hurt either of them," I snarl, fingers curling into a fist, vampire coming to the surface, "I will kill you."

With a ghostly smile at the corner of her lips, she stands, too. "I believe you," she says.

TWENTY-THREE

CHAEL WAITS FOR ME WHILE I SAY GOODBYE TO Culebra and Adelita. He follows me outside, and I feel his irritation like walking on burning hot asphalt with bare feet, impossible to ignore. He's waiting for my comment on the situation's idiocy, but honestly, I can't. In a crazy way, Janet may be the best for Culebra and Adelita.

"Well," he says, "what are you going to do about that?" He jerks a thumb back toward the bar.

I turn toward him and sigh. "What can I do?"

He stares. "What do you think? Yank her out. Send her packing back to LA. Tell Culebra to return things to the way they were."

"Why? Give me one good reason why?"

Chael does something I would never expect. His face gets purple, his arms windmill around, and he yells at me. "This is unseemly! We are vampire, the highest form of human life, and to act with such indiscretion around humans is unthinkable! If you don't stop it, I will."

Yelling at me is always a bad idea. I don't often pull the "chosen one" card, but his temper tantrum snaps me like a rubber band. Vampire rises to the surface and in one moment, I have him against my car, my hand around his neck. "You forget who you're talking to." My voice trembles with fury. "You will do nothing. You will get in your car and drive away from this place. These are my friends, my people, and if you come back here again, you forfeit your life."

Chael doesn't fight me. He grows still. He yields to the steel of my grip, but he doesn't avert his eyes either. While he's hiding his thoughts, I feel them thrusting dagger-like into my subconscious.

I subdue him, but I fear this fight is not over.

I release him and he backs away. His eyes blaze defiantly but he's not brave enough to argue, or he's not ready to.

"I don't want to fight with you, Chael," I say. "This is not a threat. What happens in Beso de la Muerte does not affect the vampire world at large. It is a microcosm not characteristic of anywhere else. Please don't challenge me on this. You will lose."

Chael straightens his shoulders, bows stiffly from the waist. "As you wish."

He turns and walks, heading to a car on the opposite side of the street. When he reaches it, a driver steps out to open the rear passenger door. The driver watches me as Chael climbs inside. He is vampire, too, and saw what happened. Chael is not happy. He likes to think of himself in charge—always.

If I'm lucky, he'll lick his wounded ego and go back to

the Middle East where he is, literally, king of his own realm.

I only hope.

———◆◆◆———

It's midnight when I get back to the office. I don't know if Frey and David will still be here, or if they've returned to David's condo. I spy David's car in the parking lot, and lights on in the office.

Frey rises first when I step inside. He raises an eyebrow at me. I shake my head. "Nothing new."

David comes around from behind the desk, paper in hand. "I think we have something."

I join them and David hands me the paper. "The car is registered to a Lorraine Simpson. Her driver license photo is on the back."

I turn the paper over and do a double take. Angular face, blue eyes, straight nose, and pointed chin.

"Duster man is a woman?"

"Unless she has a twin."

I look more closely. According to her license, she has dark hair, is 5'10", and weighs one hundred sixty pounds. The address listed is in El Cajon. I point to it. "You guys check it out?"

"Unfortunately, the license bureau didn't. It's a landfill."

Shit. "At least we have a name." I sink into a chair. "Are you running it?"

"As we speak." David returns to his place behind the desk and Frey perches on the edge, facing me.

"I checked in with John-John," he says. "He sends his love. His grandmother is recovering finally, but slowly."

I reach out and touch his knee. "Maybe that's a good thing. If he came home now, we'd not be spending much time with him," I blow out an exasperated breath. "Or have a home for him to come back to."

The computer beeps and David focuses on the screen. "We finally have something. This is from a police source. There was a Lorraine Simpson booked for involvement in a Ponzi scheme in Reno two years ago. She made a deal to give up her bosses in return for probation. Her last known address is a half-way house in LA. It's run by private contractors. We can find out where she is from someone there." He looks up at me. "We'll go first thing in the morning."

Frey nods. "While you do that, I'll stay here and see how I can put the house back in order. I can salvage most of our clothes and even put John-John's bed back together."

Plans made, fatigue settles on my shoulders like a heavy coat. I may be vampire, but I need sleep like anyone else. I yawn and stretch.

David grabs his keys from the desk top. "Let's call it a night."

"The money?"

David glances toward the filing cabinet. Our office safe is hidden behind it. "Safe and sound."

At some point, we will have to go back to the PO and pick up the rest of it. Tonight there isn't anything else we can do. As we trudge toward the parking lot, I think of Duke. I hope, wherever he is, he can hold on a little longer.

───●●●───

We're back at David's, in bed. Frey leans toward me, his lips warm against my neck, offering himself.

I snuggle closer.

Maybe it's the drama of the last few days: Duke missing, our house trashed, Culebra and Janet becoming a thing, Chael challenging me so openly in Beso de la Muerte. Whatever the reason, suddenly, vampire awakens and a primal lust overtakes me.

Frey feels it, too, the way my skin burns. His fingers trace a slow path down my body, settle between my legs. He presses gently at first, then more urgently until I rise to meet his touch. I'm reaching for him, ready, more than ready, for him to enter me.

He's over me, guiding himself in, thrusting. He lowers his head until he feels my lips at his neck. A shudder ripples his body when I break the skin. The rhythm is never interrupted, vampire and man, until we climax together, one in body and soul.

When the heat has dissipated, and the frenzy abated, Frey lays beside me, still holding me. He breathes, "I love you, Anna."

I never felt it more.

TWENTY-FOUR

DAY TEN

FREY, BLESS HIM, HAD DAVID STOP BY THE house last night so I have a change of clothes. I shower and come out of the bedroom feeling more refreshed than I have in days, when I'm met with somber expressions.

My step falters. "Uh-oh. What's up?"

David points to a seat at the breakfast bar and pours me a cup of coffee. "Checked office messages this morning. DNA results are in from the blood found in the house. It's Duke's."

I thought I prepared myself for that possibility, but it hits me hard. "Anyone else's?" I ask, hoping Duke fought back against his attacker.

David shakes his head.

"A woman gets the drop on Duke and kills him?" Sexist as it sounds, I have trouble wrapping my head around the idea. Duke wasn't big, but he kept himself in good shape. In his line of business, he had to. Clients who put their houses up as collateral for jailed relatives, who then pay them back by fleeing the jurisdiction, are often unhappy. They take it out on the bail bondsman who they begged to save their bacon weeks before.

Frey shrugs. "She may have had help."

"Don't forget," David says. "Duke knew this woman. She could get close to him because he was expecting her."

I remember Donald describing who came to Sullivan's office with Howard. He didn't realize she was a woman. If Howard and the bookie knew she was a part of the Ponzi scheme, maybe Duke did know her. Not as a mastermind, but maybe as a fellow investor.

"Let's hit the road." I toss Frey my car keys. "We'll call you with what we find at the half-way house."

He leans down and kisses my cheek. "See you when you get back."

We leave the condo together, and David and I part company with Frey in the parking lot. I'm not looking forward to another trek to LA, but we have a definite goal.

Half-way houses are seldom located in "good" neighborhoods—where the NIMBY syndrome is alive and well. This one proves to be the exception. David and I exchange surprised glances when the address we are directed to turns out to be in a nice, middle-class neighborhood of stucco ranch houses with neatly trim yards and lots of trees. There are families strolling the sidewalks, children playing in front yards, and joggers out for morning runs.

Not what we expected.

We approach the front door and ring.

A small grated window set in the door swings open and a face peers out at us.

"No solicitors," a voice says. "Whatever you're selling, we don't want any."

David pulls a small leather case from his pocket and flips it open. He holds it up. "Not soliciting. Looking for someone who lived here. We're insurance investigators."

The pair of eyes examines the card. "Who are you looking for?"

David unfolds the driver's license photo and holds it up. "Lorraine Simpson."

There's a scoffing sound. "You wasted a trip. Lorraine hasn't been here in a year."

David nods. "We understand that, but it is important that we find her. Could we come in and talk to whoever's in charge?"

The window closes, and David and I are left standing on the porch. Long seconds tick by. Finally we hear the lock turn, and the door swings open.

I don't know what surprises me more—that it's a young woman in jeans and a turtleneck sweater, or that she's wearing the headpiece and veil of a Catholic nun. Maybe that's the reason they live here. We passed a Catholic church a block away. A church affiliation may have smoothed the way.

She motions us to come in.

David looks as surprised as I do, but we pull ourselves together enough to follow her inside.

She closes the door behind us and holds out a hand. "Sister Mary Claire," she says. "How may I help you?"

David accepts her hand first. "We're hoping you can help us find Lorraine Simpson," he says.

Sister Mary Claire leads us into a sitting room where another young girl is busy vacuuming. "Rosie, you can finish up later." She waits until the girl has left and closes the door behind her. "Why are you looking for her?"

"She's in trouble, but you might already know that."

The young nun frowns, but doesn't ask for details. She has a pretty, no-nonsense face that, I imagine, has no problem making sure rules are followed in her house. She gestures to the couch and, once David and I are settled, sinks into a chair across from us.

"She isn't one of our success stories," she says. "She was sent here as a condition of her probation but stayed only long enough to cause trouble for everyone. I was about to notify her parole officer when she disappeared. She never gave us a chance."

"Do you have any idea where she went?" I ask.

When Sister Mary Claire turns toward me, I see a flash of—something—in her eyes. As if she recognizes what I am. She recovers quickly.

"I have the address of an elderly aunt who lives in San Diego," she continues, the presentiment of awareness gone from her eyes. "I'll get it for you. Though when I called looking for her, I was told Lorraine hadn't been in touch for months. When I told her Lorraine was missing, she was genuinely concerned. She said her biggest regret was that she didn't do more to help her niece after Lorraine's parents passed."

She leaves her chair to cross to a big roll-top desk set against the far wall. She rummages in a drawer and pulls out a Rolodex. It's been a long time since I've seen one; most people use computers to keep files now. She walks her fingers along the dividers until she finds the letter she's looking for, sorts the cards, and pulls one out. Jotting the information on a slip of paper, she hands it to me.

"Here," she says, glancing at the card. "Genny Davis is the only contact I have." She sighs. "Lorraine isn't a bad person. She lacks discipline, and someone to believe in her," she adds with a hint of disappointment, "I had hoped it would be us."

David and I stand up, and Sister Marie Claire leads us back into the hallway. She opens the door but touches my arm. I let David go out ahead of me to turn back.

"I've known your kind before," she says, kindly. "If you need someone to talk to, my door is always open. The church is far more tolerant than you might imagine."

I don't know what to say. As a rule, humans don't recognize me as vampire. If they do, I expect fear or disgust to be the reaction. This catches me completely off guard and confirms that I hadn't imagined what I'd felt before.

I want to ask what gave me away, but David is waiting outside the door, so I simply nod and join him.

"What did she say to you?" David asks as we head for the car.

"Nothing," I reply. "She wishes us luck."

TWENTY-FIVE

I MULL OVER SISTER MARY CLAIRE'S WORDS AS we drive back to San Diego. It's the first time a human has made a remark like that to me. We vampires have tried very hard to keep our existence secret, except for those who volunteer to be hosts. Frankly, I never asked one how they came to know about us.

Then Janet found out.

Maybe we aren't such a secret.

I check in with Frey. He's making head-way in the house and reports there isn't as much damage as we first thought. After righting upended furniture, replacing mattresses, and repairing John-John's bed, the only things he had to trash were ripped cushions, remarking that was probably done more for effect than anything else. Luckily (or maybe not so luckily), he had some experience with removing blood stains. Except for a couple of small accent rugs in the living room that he also threw out, he's managed to scrub away most of Duke's blood.

Duke's blood.

GPS directs us to the address Sister Mary Claire gave us. It's an area known as Encanto, a mixed neighborhood primed for urbanization, although it hasn't yet reached 312 Thrush Street, a tiny, box-like house on a swath of grass. The yard is well-cared for, and an American flag flies on a pole from the front porch. A mailbox with "Davis" stenciled on the side and "312" sits at the edge of the sidewalk. There's no garage and no cars parked on the street, either. We park across the street.

Before David and I can discuss this interview, the front door opens. An elderly lady walks out, down the stairs and up the sidewalk. She looks in her eighties, tiny, 4'5" tall, wearing a long, dark coat with embroidered flowers on the lapel. A cloth hat set at a jaunty angle on a tangle of bright red curls. Her oversize glasses perch on a snub nose under which lips accented by bright red lipstick are pursed in a determined frown. She clutches a shiny black patent leather handbag to her chest with one hand, pulls a rolling grocery cart filled with plastic trash bags behind her with the other.

She may be elderly, but her appearance is important to her. Her bag and shoes match, as do her hat and coat. Her lipstick was carefully applied, no smudges. Her attention to detail gives me hope she'll help in finding her niece.

I glance at David. "Aunt Genny?"

"Cart looks full," he answers. "Wonder where she's taking it?"

"Let's find out."

We wait for her to move further up the block before following. She stops at a bus stop not far from the house.

We stop, too, hesitating. "What now? Go back for the car?" I ask.

We glance behind us to see a bus approaching. "No time," David answers.

There are a half dozen people waiting along with Lorraine's aunt. We take our places at the end of the line. Neither of us know what bus fare is nowadays, and we don't know where we're headed, so we pay five bucks each for transfers.

We take seats in the back, allowing us to watch where Lorraine's aunt gets off. The bus heads west from 63rd and Brooklyn. After ten minutes, she exits at the Euclid Station and heads for the 11th and Broadway Station. We follow. These are popular routes and we blend in with the crowd. We're on the next bus when we recognize where we're headed. Downtown.

So far, so good.

She gets off at Broadway and Union. Familiar territory for us. Duke's office is just a few blocks away. We're perplexed when Lorraine's aunt heads straight for his building.

David and I hang back for a moment, not wanting to give ourselves away, but here in the bustle of downtown in early afternoon, we hurry to catch up. The security guard in Duke's building is so busy answering questions for a pretty young woman that he doesn't look up when Lorraine's aunt comes through the door. She walks right past him and heads for the elevator.

We head for the stairs. If we miscalculate, and she isn't heading for Duke's office, we'll have to wait for her to return downstairs and keep following.

We beat her to the 8th floor and stand in the stairwell until we hear the elevator ding. She's the only one who exits. We slip into the hallway once she's past.

Duke's office is in the corner at the end of the hall. She's been here before because she doesn't look at the doors to find his number. She stops in front of it and knocks three times.

"It's open." says a voice inside.

As soon as the door opens, David and I rush.

She gasps when we push her and her cart inside, and slam the door behind us. She lets go of the cart and it rolls to a stop against the wall beside the door.

Lorraine and Duke jump to their feet from their perches on opposite corners of Duke's desk.

"What the fuck?" Duke says. "Where did you two come from?"

In two steps, I'm across the office and twist Lorraine Simpson's arm behind her back. I'm about to break out the handcuffs when Duke snatches me back.

"What the fuck are you doing, Anna?" he asks. "Stop before you break her arm."

I look at Duke. He doesn't have a mark or bruise on his face.

Lorraine's aunt rushes at me. "Let her go," she yells, beating at me with clenched fists.

She barely comes to my chest, but she flails at me as though she were a giant.

I let go of Lorraine and pin Genny's arms at her sides.

David, gun in hand, stands by the door indecisively.

Duke approaches and pries Genny Davis out of my arms. Gently, he steers her toward a chair and lowers her into it. He turns toward us.

"I guess I owe you an explanation."

"You guess?" I snap back. "We're worried to death about you. My house was ransacked. We found blood—your blood—all over the place. We thought you died." I jerk a thumb in Lorraine's direction. "We thought she killed you."

Duke gestures to David. "Put your gun away," he says. "I'll explain. Lorraine hasn't hurt me. She's protecting me."

"What about the blood we found?" David asks, gun still pointed in Lorraine's direction. "It was yours, that's verified. Listen, Duke. If she has a hold over you, tell us. We're here now. We can protect you."

"I'm not threatening, Duke," Lorraine says.

It's the first time we hear her voice. A low, husky, Kathleen Turner kind of voice. It makes every head in the room swivel towards her, mine included.

Duke puts his hand over David's and forces the gun down. "She's right."

David holsters the Glock.

"Explain," David says.

"It better be good," I add. "You trashed my place."

Duke winces. "Sorry. I had to make it look real. I hope we didn't do too much damage."

"Really?" My voice rags with indignation as a vision of John-John's bed flashes through my head. "You ransacked my stepson's room."

"What about your blood?" David pipes in. "How did you manage to get so much of it over so many surfaces? We expected your bloodless corpse to show up in a landfill or wash up on the beach."

"Lorraine took care of that." He sounds proud. "She worked as a nurse's aide for a while and knows how to draw blood. She extracted about a pint and a half from me, and we made sure to spread it around. It's amazing how far a little blood can go."

He's too cheerful. I bite my tongue to keep from throttling that smile off his face. "If you don't want to lose any more blood," I say slowly and with enough menace in my tone to make him stiffen, "tell us what the fuck is going on."

"Can I ask you a question first?"

"Make it quick."

"Did you find the money?"

David and I exchange glances. "It's safe," he says.

Duke's shoulders relax. "I knew I could count on you." He half turns to Lorraine. "I told you they'd come through."

Lorraine grins back at him. "We're out of the woods." She bends down to her aunt. "Did you bring what I asked?"

Genny nods and points to her rolling cart on the floor beside the door.

Lorraine kisses her forehead and smiles. She rummages inside one of the trash bags. When she straightens and turns toward us, we're staring into the muzzle of a sawed off, double-barreled shotgun.

We all react differently. David draws his weapon, but Lorraine anticipates his move and jabs the shotgun barrel into his chest, stopping him.

Duke's mouth falls open. "What are you doing?"

I want to rush her. A shotgun blast would be only a painful inconvenience to me, but would betray what I am, which has to be a last resort. Aunt Genny, sits quietly, proud as she watches her niece.

Lorraine addresses her. "Aunt Genny, take David's gun, will you?"

The elderly woman quickly jumps to her feet and expertly disarms David—a wonder to watch since she barely comes to his waist. When Lorraine turns the shotgun on me, she stands behind me and pats me down, finding the small .38 snubby I have clipped to my belt, and removes it. She takes David's gun and places it in the same grocery bag from which Lorraine removed the shotgun. She hangs onto my gun.

"Now," Lorraine says, turning to face us. "Down to business. Where's the eight mill?"

Eight mill?

"Sorry to disappoint you," I say. "There was not eight million dollars in that PO box."

Lorraine looks at Duke, who sputters, "What do you mean? There was supposed to be eight million."

Lorraine skewers him with a dark frown. "Are you lying to me?" She pokes the gun into his rib cage. "Have you hidden some of the money? I swear I'll shoot your friends one by one until you tell me where the rest of the money is." She turns the gun in my direction. "I'll start with her."

David steps between us. "He's not lying," he says. "If you shoot us, you'll never know where to find the money, not even the two million we have."

"Two million?" Duke sputters again. "There's supposed to be eight in that box."

"Maybe," David says. "But whoever mailed the money didn't know how many envelopes that post office box could hold."

Lorraine pokes Duke again. "You idiot." She whirls on David. "Where's the rest?"

"Being held for pick up by the owner of the PO box."

"Who has to show identification," I add. "Shooting Duke isn't the smartest thing you could do, unless you can come up with another man to impersonate Sullivan."

"And the two million you have?"

David and I remain silent. Lorraine looks at Duke. He looks away but I can see that Lorraine knows Duke knows where we stashed the money. He probably told her. He's the one who had the safe installed in our office.

Lorraine takes a step back and turns to her aunt. "What do you think, Aunt Genny? What should I do?"

Without pause, she answers, "Shoot those two." She jabs a finger at David and me. "You don't need them. Take that one," indicating Duke, "and let's get to that post office."

I almost laugh remembering how Sister Mary Claire had the impression Lorraine's aunt would have been a good influence. More likely, she's where Lorraine inherited her criminal proclivities.

Lorraine cocks her head. Outside the door, the murmur of voices. It's a little after one and people are returning to their offices from lunch. "Can't do it here," she says, hefting the shotgun. "Too noisy. We need to leave them here for now. Come back tonight and finish then." She turns to Duke. "I'm sure you must have a pair of handcuffs or two lying around the office, don't you?"

Duke nods, conflicting emotions playing across his face. This is not the way he expected things to unfold. He moves slowly around the desk, mindful of the shotgun Lorraine has at his chest. He opens a drawer, but before he can reach inside, she's moved around and shoves the gun barrel against his neck.

"You don't have a gun in that drawer, do you?"

His head shakes woodenly.

She peers inside, then motions for him to proceed.

He pulls out two pairs of handcuffs and tosses them on the desk.

Lorraine shoves him down into the desk chair. "Aunt Genny, watch him. If he moves, shoot him." She chuckles. "Don't kill him, of course. We still need him for the money."

Genny smiles and points my .38 at his crotch.

She's one tough nut.

Lorraine motions for me and David to move to the back of the office. I'm tempted to rush her, but Genny would likely shoot Duke, and I have a lot of questions for him. I don't fight when Lorraine positions David and me on the floor behind the desk, each of us with our feet facing opposite walls, the tops of our heads almost touching. She locks our hands behind us with the cuffs. I have to stifle a smile. If she'd made us lie side by side, David would see me break free. This way, he won't.

When she finishes handcuffing us, she rummages in Duke's middle drawer. She evidently finds what she's looking for, because the next thing I hear is ripping fabric. Then she's on her knees beside me, yanking my head back so she can force a hunk of material in my mouth before wrapping another around my head. She catches my hair in the knot she ties in the back, pulling it so tight I wince with pain.

That brings a chuckle.

I'll thank her for it later.

She moves to David. I hear him mumble, "You'll never get away with this, bitch," before his words cut off.

Lorraine moves away. I can see her legs and feet as she approaches her aunt.

"Are you ready, Auntie?"

She must nod, because Duke is brought to his feet. Genny says, "Lorraine, honey, do we have a car?"

"We do," Lorraine answers. "Duke's parked in the underground employee lot. We'll take the stairs. No cameras."

Duke hasn't said a word since Lorraine voiced her intentions. I wonder how in the hell he got involved with her, and where she fits in the Ponzi scheme. Does he know about who she's killed?

I can't see what they're doing, but I hear the cart rustle with the grocery bags. I assume Lorraine is hiding the shotgun. Lorraine says, "Don't worry. You'll see them again."

Her meaning is clear.

I hear Duke grunt as though she's rammed the .38 hard into his stomach.

The door opens. Closes.

Alone at last.

TWENTY-SIX

I BREAK THE HANDCUFFS APART WITH NO PROB-lem. A quick jerk and the chain separates. My hands are free. I pull at the gag, forgetting the hair caught in the knot, and yelp as a quarter-size chunk of hair pulls out by the roots. Fuck. Vampire hair grows very slowly. I'm not sure if hair pulled out by the roots grows back at all.

I'm rubbing the back of my head, cursing Lorraine, forgetting the predicament we're in until a squirming David refocuses my attention. He tries to see what's happening behind him, arching his back and grunting noises as if asking, "What the fuck?"

I move to his side, untie his gag, and pull it off.

"How did you get free?" he asks, eyeing the cuff bracelets encircling my wrists.

I shrug and lie. "Must have been defective," I say. "I gave a good yank and they broke apart."

"My pocket," David says.

I raise an eyebrow.

"My pocket. I have a key to unlock the cuffs."

He rolls on his side and I slide a hand into his back pocket. Lorraine missed the key when she frisked him. Or maybe not. She could never have guessed I'd break out of a pair of steel cuffs. With them on, neither one of us could have reached the key. In a second, he's free, too.

"Damn, those were tight." David rubs his wrists. "They don't have much of a head start on us." He lumbers to his feet. "We know where they're headed."

"One problem. We left the car at good old Aunt Genny's." Then I remember. "Frey," I say. "I'll call Frey and have him come pick us up." I've got the phone in my hand and his cell dialed before David finishes massaging some feeling back into his wrists.

It's about fifteen minutes before Frey pulls up in front of Duke's building. David jumps in back, and I ride shotgun. I fill in Frey in as he heads for the freeway. Duke working with Lorraine surprises him.

"Do you think she's the one who killed Howard and the bookie?" Frey asks. "Sarah Sullivan? Duke doesn't have a clue?"

"Either that, or it was Aunt Genny," David remarks dryly.

I chuckle but shake my head. "I don't think so. He was genuinely surprised when she turned on us—and him. We never got a chance to ask him how he got that money. Up until two days ago, he had me and David chasing it." I shoot David a sideways glance. "I take it you never saw Lorraine before today. She wasn't part of the LLC with you and Duke?"

"If she was, Duke never told me. To be honest, I never

asked. I had Gloria's three mill to invest and I thought the other five was Duke's."

Frey says, "You invested *Gloria's* money?"

His tone was the same as mine when David told me, disbelief tinged with astonishment.

Color creeps up David's neck. "My money is all tied up—real estate, hedge funds. The deal sounded too good to pass. I manage Gloria's portfolio. She received a good chunk of change from the sale of some foreign movie rights. Cash. If this deal was for real, she'd have almost doubled her investment. It seemed a no-brainer."

Too good to be true. I keep quiet. I'm sure David beat himself over the head with that stick too many times to count.

Something dawns. I swivel to face David. "Lorraine never pressed us on where we stashed the two million."

His eyebrows jump. "You're right. I wonder why?"

Shit. "She's sure Duke knows." I bark, "Turn around, Frey. Duke knows the combination of our office safe. I bet they're going to stop at the office before heading to LA."

Frey pulls off at the next exit and swings back toward San Diego.

I can't believe I didn't think of this sooner. If we're lucky, we may catch them at the office. A drive by confirms they are inside. Duke's big Escalade is parked in David's spot. We can see the top of Aunt Genny's head in the back seat. Frey drives on, pulling over once we're out of her sight.

I open the Jag's glove box. It's long and deep. I keep a second .38 behind a false back. It's illegal as hell but useful in times like this. It's loaded, too, but only five rounds.

I hand it to Frey. "You hang on to this. Keep an eye on Genny. If Lorraine and Duke are inside, and we can't get the drop on them, we'll need an element of surprise—you."

He nods.

Frey lets us out, and David and I head for the rear of the building. We make our way along the terraces that span the back of each office. There are five in all—three have drawn blinds against the harsh reflection of sun on water. The fourth is luckily vacant as we sneak by, but our blinds are open, and there's no place to conceal ourselves once we step onto the deck.

I motion for David to stop and wait out of sight on the neighbor's terrace while I sneak closer to ours to peek inside. Lorraine and Duke slide the file cabinet aside, revealing the safe. Duke argues he doesn't know the combination. Lorraine isn't buying. She hits Duke in the side of his head with the gun's butt.

Duke staggers, tripping over one of the desk chairs, and goes down hard.

Lorraine hovers over him, gun above her head, her back to me.

I don't wait. I can't be stealthy.

I take a step back and ram the slider with my shoulder.

The force doesn't shatter the safety glass, but rather sends it crashing into the room in one piece.

Lorraine whirls around.

Duke takes the opportunity to yank her ankle, bless him.

She falls face first onto the floor, the gun skittering loose.

David jumps the rail between the terraces and holds Lorraine on the floor while I go to Duke.

Blood trickles from a cut on the side of his head where Lorraine hit him. His mood is pure fury. He shakes my hand off and scrabbles to Lorraine.

"You bitch," he snarls.

I call Frey.

"We've got Lorraine," I say. "You still have Genny in sight?"

"She jumped out of the car when she heard the crash, but she hasn't moved. Should I bring her in?"

"Do it."

David wrestles Lorraine to her feet and shoves her into a desk chair. He breaks out a nylon double-tie handcuff and yanks her hands together. There's no question why he chose those instead of our steel cuffs. He makes sure they're as tight around her wrists as his cuffs were around his.

Lorraine yelps, "You'll cut off my circulation."

"Where was that concern when you handcuffed me?" He moves around to face her. "As long as you stay still and don't struggle, you'll be fine."

The door opens and Frey comes in holding a squirming Genny tight in his arms. He lowers her to the floor. "Where'd you find this one?"

David gets her to a chair and has her bound before she has a chance to compose herself. She lets loose with a stream of invective that startles us all, most of it directed at Lorraine and that she let herself be caught.

Lorraine says nothing in her defense. It amazes me how this diminutive person has such an effect on her. I understand why she's maintained her distance.

Duke is quiet since his outburst at Lorraine. He sits on the floor, head bowed. David, Frey and I form a phalanx around him.

I level my face with his. "What's going on Duke?" I ask quietly. "Where did you get all that money and how—" I jerk a thumb in Lorraine's direction, "—does she figure into it?"

"Don't tell them anything, Duke," Lorraine says. "We can still make this work."

Duke shoots her an exasperated look. "Make what work? You were going to kill me once you got the money. You think I'd trust anything you say now?" He scowls at her before turning back to me. "She was a friend of Howard's."

"A friend? Did you know she was with him at Sullivan's right before they were killed? Hell, she may have been there when they were killed." I turn to Lorraine. "What about it?"

Lorraine's lips are drawn tight, her jaw clenched. She stares at me, a defiant lift to her chin.

I focus on Duke. "The money? How'd you get it?"

"I didn't. I got a note from Sullivan saying I'd find eight million dollars, our investment, addressed to me in a PO box in LA. We were supposed to meet and go after it together but he never showed."

"We didn't find the key among Sullivan's things," David says. "We found it in a file cabinet in a police lockup."

"We thought it was a safety deposit box key," I add, "until David found a receipt for a post office box among his papers at Sarah Sullivan's apartment."

"She just let you have it?"

David shrugs. "She didn't know I took it. I don't think she had any idea what her husband was involved in. It didn't matter. She was killed right after Anna and I went to speak to her." He eyeballs Lorraine. "Your handiwork?"

She presses her lips together and glares at us. We're not getting anything from this one.

"Let's piece together what we know without her," David says. "We know she was with Howard when he visited Sullivan with Taylor. She knew about the scam before you did, Duke." He stares at Lorraine. "Were you Howard's mistress? You meant something to him or he wouldn't tell you what was going on. Things begin to unravel. Sullivan worked with Taylor, and when he found out he was dead, he must have panicked. Taylor was the money man between him and Oswald. He didn't know how much Oswald knew or if Taylor ever divulged his identity to Oswald. As far as he knew, Taylor made the payments as arranged, just enough to keep the ship afloat and allow Oswald to keep up appearances."

Duke shakes his head. "Why go after me?"

Some of the dominoes are falling. "Howard was your nephew," I say, taking up where David left off. "Taylor's killer wanted you out of the way while he went after Howard because he knew Sullivan and Howard were in on the scam together…not the sporting ticket thing, but the skimming.

Unfortunately, Howard was killed for information he didn't have. Sullivan was the one who knew where the money was."

I focus on Lorraine. "When you found out how much money was involved, did you decide then to cut Howard out and go for the money yourself or did that happen later? Was it a pleasant surprise when Howard showed up dead?"

Duke jumps to his feet. "Is that why Taylor came to visit me? The man he was with—another friend of yours?" He turns to David. "I had a message from Clayton Oswald the morning I was attacked and Taylor killed. I never had a chance to return his call."

"The newspapers say Oswald claims to know nothing of the Ponzi scheme," I say. "He may be telling the truth. Taylor's murder was the incident that made Sullivan keep the eight million he planned to pass on to Oswald. He got a PO box and mailed the cash. Get away money, maybe."

Duke shakes his head, passing a hand over his face. "Why would Sullivan send all that money to me in care of the PO box?" he asks.

I snap my fingers. "Maybe the answer is in one of the envelopes. We'll need to get a phony ID made in Sullivan's name so we can collect the rest of the money."

Lorraine's sharp intake of breath makes us all swivel. She straightens in her chair and shoots me a poisonous look. "How are you going to do that?" she snaps. "The box is in Sullivan's name."

I ignore her question and pose one to Duke. "Duke, you still have your contact for this sort of thing?"

He grins. "I'll get him on the line now. He should have the ID ready soon." He pulls out his cell, but pauses. "Who's going to be Sullivan?"

"It can't be David," I say. "People still recognize him from his football days. Even if they didn't, someone in that post office is bound to notice Sullivan was not six-foot-six and two hundred fifty pounds."

"What about me?" Frey says.

I forgot Frey was with us. I throw him a guilty smile. "Are you sure you want to get involved?"

"I already am," he says.

"Okay. Frey will be Sullivan."

Duke places his call, exchanges greetings, then makes an appointment for a special rush printing job. He disconnects and says to Frey, "He's at the shop now. We can go over anytime."

"David and I will stay here with the girls," I say, waving a hand in Lorraine and Genny's direction. "You'll need cash. How much?"

Duke thinks a minute. "For a rush job, twenty-five hundred should do it."

David turns Lorraine and Genny around in their chairs so they can't see the safe combination. I push the envelopes aside to reach our cash, withdraw the funds, close the safe door, and spin the lock.

"Here's three thousand." I glance at my watch. "It's too late to make it to LA tonight. We can start first thing in the morning." I go to the desk and write out Sullivan's address. "I hope he used his apartment address when he rented the box. It's the only one I have."

Duke takes the note and sticks it in his pocket. He nods toward Lorraine and Genny. "What do we do about these two?"

I shrug. "Sit on them until tomorrow. We'll decide then."

Frey brushes my cheek with a butterfly kiss and hands me my gun. "Be careful of the little one," he says. "She bites."

TWENTY-SEVEN

DAY ELEVEN

DUKE'S FORGER DOES EXCELLENT WORK. THE
phony driver's license with Sullivan's info and Frey's picture
even has the hologram. He slips it into his wallet. I make sure
the note from the post office to come pick up the rest of the
mail in person is in my jacket pocket.

David stays at the office with Lorraine and Genny, after
letting them take an escorted potty break and feeding them a
Mickey D's sausage muffin and water, Frey, Duke and I head
back to LA.

We decide that Frey and I will go into the post office while
Duke stays with the car. We don't know how many envelopes
we'll be hauling out or what kind of questions we'll get from
the postal employees. We hope that none of the envelopes
tore and exposed the contents. Otherwise, we may have local
police and the FBI waiting for us.

"Assuming we get the money, what are we doing with

Lorraine and her aunt?" Frey asks.

He's driving and I'm riding shotgun. "I think Lorraine is still on probation. She's in violation for leaving the county. We have her gun. We could turn her in."

"What about her aunt?" Duke leans forward. "She's a tough cookie. I can see her coming after us for revenge." He pauses. "What if we offer her some money? I doubt there's much love lost between her and her niece. She may not care that Lorraine is going back to prison as long as she gets a cut of the money."

"You're keeping it?" I ask Duke.

He looks at me in disbelief. "Why shouldn't we? We invested it. I feel for others who lose their nut. I don't understand why Sullivan wanted me to get our money back, but he did, and I say, 'Thank you, Harold.'"

"It wasn't about Howard stealing half a million from you, was it?"

Duke looks abashed. "I couldn't tell you the truth. As soon as I heard my nephew was dead, I knew I couldn't put you in any more danger."

Frey says, "How did a bookie become the money man for your investment? Duke, what were you thinking?"

Duke frowns. "It was a good investment. I don't know how Sullivan became the money man. Talbot was the only one who could answer that and he's dead."

It's about nine when we pull into the post office parking lot. There's already a line forming outside the door, so we wait until everyone is inside. Frey and I exit the car, and Duke takes

Frey's place behind the wheel.

"I'll be right over there," he points to a parking space close to the door.

Frey and I nod and watch as he backs into the space, ready to pull out when we return.

"Why do I feel like we're about to rob a bank?" I mumble.

Frey grins and holds open the door. "Here we go."

There are ten people in line and, as is common in most busy post offices, only two windows open. I shift nervously back and forth from one leg to another until Frey puts his hands on my shoulders.

"Relax. We're only here to pick up mail. Not a big deal."

I suck in a breath and stop fidgeting. The line moves at a snail's pace, but we're finally called to the window.

I hand Frey the note.

"Good morning," he says, chipper and calm. He hands over the note. "Sorry it's taken me so long to get to this. I've been out of town."

The woman behind the counter responds to Frey's smile with hers. She scans the note. "I need to see some identification, Mr. Sullivan," she says.

Frey takes the license out of his wallet and hands it to her.

She examines the license, hands it back. "All right. If I remember correctly, you have quite a bit of mail. I'll meet you at the back door, around the corner." She places her "back in five minutes" sign up, greeted by the impatient sighs of everyone in line.

"Why would she know Sullivan has a lot of mail?" I whisper as Frey and I make our way to the back door. Alarms go off in my head. "This is a big post office. How would she recognize one customer's name?"

My skin crawls with visions of cops swarming. The back door opens, and she's alone with a handcart full of manila envelopes. I wilt with relief. I motion Duke to bring the car over.

"What do you have?" the employee asks, fingering one of the envelopes. "Some kind of mail order business?"

Frey and I haul armfuls of envelopes out of the cart and stack them into the trunk.

"Yes." Duke answers, pitching in. "It's very successful."

"I can see."

We empty the cart and she turns to wheel it back inside. "We can put mail in your box again," she says, then laughs. "Unless, of course, this is the norm."

Frey shakes his head. "I'm sure it won't be. I think our luck is played out."

"That happens." She opens the door and pushes the cart through. "Have a good day."

None of us say a word until we're back on the road. I scan the rear view mirrors, expecting flashing lights and sirens to appear. When we make it to the freeway, my shoulders unbunch.

Duke peers behind him, too. "I think we did it," he says, releasing a breath.

I lean my head back on the seat. "Next problem," I say. "Where do we put the money?"

"I have a basement safe in my house," Duke answers. "It's

big enough to fit it all in."

I swivel. "You have a basement? We didn't see it when we went to your house."

"You're not supposed to," he answers. "The stairs are hidden behind a false wall in the pantry."

Frey and I exchange amused looks. "You must keep most of your money there," he says. "You don't believe in banks?"

Duke shrugs. "I prefer to manage my own assets."

"You make no interest," I point out. "Shouldn't you be investing?"

Duke snorts. "I just tried that, remember? Look how it turned out."

Can't argue with him.

TWENTY-EIGHT

IT'S EARLY AFTERNOON WHEN WE RETURN TO the office.

As soon as we walk in empty handed, David groans. "There was trouble. You didn't get the money."

Lorraine was slouching in her chair, and at that, she perks up. "I knew you couldn't pull it off. This has all been for nothing. Let me and my aunt go now, and I won't press charges against you for false imprisonment."

"That is funny, Lorraine," I say. "But you're going back to jail. We already called the cops to collect you. Being here in San Diego violates your parole." I walk over to the desk where her shotgun lays. "Possessing a firearm ensures you won't get another chance at parole for some time."

Genny is watching us, eyes narrow. "What about me? How will you explain tying me up?"

Duke grins and walks over. He cuts her free and takes her arm. "You're going to take a walk with me. Say goodbye to your niece."

Lorraine gives a startled cry. "Aunt Genny, You can't let them do this to me."

"Whatever can I do?" Genny turns from a pit bull into a Pomeranian. "I can't get myself arrested. I'm an old lady. I'll never last in prison."

Duke begins to escort her outside. I stop him with a hand on his arm. "Be careful. Remember, she wanted to shoot me and David in your office. She would have, too, if she had half a chance. Don't let this poor old lady routine fool you."

Duke's mouth forms a thin, hard line. "I haven't forgotten. I know how to handle this. Will you three be all right until the police get here for Lorraine?"

I nod. "We'll be in touch as soon as she's taken."

Duke leaves with an acquiescent Genny, and Lorraine's eyes widen with disbelief as she watches the door close behind them.

"You didn't call the police, did you?" she says after a moment.

"We did," I reply.

"What's to prevent me from telling the cops about the money you have in your safe? How will you explain that?"

"We won't need to," Frey answers. He points to the slider lying on the floor. "You broke in to rob us. We're bounty hunters. We are often in possession of large amounts of cash. Besides, we know most of the cops in town. They'll take our word over yours anytime."

I see the wheels turning in Lorraine's head.

"What is it, Lorraine?" I ask. "Do you have something to

tell us? You don't have very long before the police arrive. We told them we had you cuffed, so there is no rush, but they will get here eventually."

Lorraine looks back and forth between me and Frey, studying us, as if deciding who to appeal to. She decides.

"You look reasonable. Can't you talk sense into your wife? If I'm arrested, you won't know who was behind the Ponzi scheme. Believe me, he's still out there. He killed Taylor and probably the others as well. He won't stop until he gets the rest of the money Sullivan hid from Oswald."

Frey smiles, amused. "You appeal to the wrong person," he says. "You have to convince David and Anna."

David plants himself in front of Lorraine. "I don't believe you know any more than we do. If you did, you wouldn't have chased Duke."

"I didn't *chase* Duke," she spits. "I was told to stick to him. After you spoke with Sarah Sullivan and she couldn't help, you found something on your own. You moved too fast for him to intercept you after your first trip to the post office."

"Who told you to stick with Duke?" Impatience sharpens my words.

"If I told you that, you wouldn't need to call off the police."

"We're not calling off the police," I say. "Whether you tell us who this mystery man is or not, we did pretty well on our own. We'll figure it out."

She shakes her head. "No. You won't. Believe me, you don't want this man after you. He won't give up until he has the money or you're dead. All three of you."

I can't believe I didn't see it before. "You were willing to take that chance." I move to stand beside David. "You and your aunt were going to take the money from Duke and run. After all, two million in the hand…"

Lorraine looks up at me. "Going after the post office money was too big a risk. I made him believe Duke was still looking for it. Since he would be dead, he couldn't argue the point."

Duke came back in time to hear Lorraine's remark. He scoffs. "You are a peach, you know that, Lorraine?"

David jerks his head toward the door. "Did you take care of Genny?" he asks.

Duke smiles. "Sent her home in a taxi smiling like she found a fifty thousand dollar lottery ticket." He glares at Lorraine. "Which, in a way, she did."

"What?" Lorraine straightens. "You gave her money?" She struggles against her restraints. "Why? What did she tell you?"

Duke peers out the front window. "I'm disappearing for a few minutes," he says. "I don't recognize those officers, but if they recognize me, I'll have to explain where I was for the last few days."

David sends him out the back and across the neighbors' verandas the same way we entered.

When the officers arrive, I expect Lorraine to raise hell, kick, and scream. She surprises us by following quietly to the awaiting police car. Maybe she thinks the money is out there somewhere. David and I surrender her rifle and answer a few questions about the broken slider, and how we caught her breaking into our safe. Since they know she's a parole violator, the entire process takes less than fifteen minutes.

Once Lorraine is in police custody, David, Frey, Duke and I pull chairs to the desk to determine our next move.

"Now what?" David asks.

David doesn't know that we have the money. I fill him in and watch the tension drain from his shoulders. "It's in Duke's safe at home."

Duke says, "We did it." He looks pleased with himself. He dusts his hands together in a good riddance gesture and grins. "This was in one of the envelopes."

He hands David a folded paper. I watch David smooth it out and read. When he finishes, he grins up at Duke. "That explains one thing."

I nod. "Sullivan knew he'd become a target. He returned our money with the hope we'd find out who was after him. Unfortunately, we didn't get this in time to keep him and Howard alive."

Duke continues, "Guess what Genny told me?"

"The name of the guy Lorraine says is after the money?"

"Not quite. She doesn't know a name but she described who came to see Lorraine after she left the half-way house."

"Let me guess," David says. "Tall. Six-two, two-twenty five. Blonde hair, brown eyes. No distinguishing marks."

Duke shakes his head. "Female. Fifty-ish. Attractive. Walks with a limp."

David and I do a double take. "Kitty DelMonico?" I say

at the same time David says, "Howard's wife?"

After the shock wears off, I think about it. "We assumed it was a man, and Lorraine never corrected us."

David shakes his head. "Kitty DelMonico is no killer," he says. "I'd be willing to stake my life on it."

Duke nods. "Normally, I agree with David. I've known Kitty for years. If she found out what Howard was involved in, she'd have a strong motive to find the money. He already squandered her inheritance. Her ranch is mortgaged to the hilt. She is permanently disabled because of his recklessness."

"He caused the accident that hurt her?"

Duke lets out a harsh breath. "It wasn't an accident. He got in deep with a loan shark. When he sent a collector, Howard wasn't home, but Kitty was. The guy was told to deliver a message. He did with a ball-peen hammer and broke both of her knee caps. She kicked Howard out after that, and he came to work for me."

I have a tough time picturing Kitty as the mastermind behind four murders. "I can't see it. I can't see Kitty killing four people, no matter how angry she was at her ex."

"Kitty's a lot tougher than you think." Duke says. "She's has to be, but I agree that she's no killer. When Taylor came to my office, he was with a man, but that's not to say he wasn't working for Kitty."

"What do we do now?" I ask. "Duke, you and David have all your money back. Howard's dead. Lorraine goes back to jail. Do you think you could reason with Kitty to call off her hired muscle?"

"Are you serious?" David says. "This hired muscle killed four people. You don't think he should pay for that?"

"I think we need to speak with Kitty," Duke says. "I don't know what she promised him, but I'm willing to bet that asking him to stop now will not change anything but maybe get her killed, too."

I sigh. "I guess we pay Kitty a visit."

TWENTY-NINE

IT'S LATE AFTERNOON NOW AND SINCE DAVID, Frey and Duke haven't had anything to eat all day, food is the first concern. There are plenty of restaurants down the street from our offices in Seaport Village. I send the three of them with the excuse that I need to check with the police about the break-in at our house. Frey says he'll bring something back for me with a wink and nod unseen by David and Duke. I kiss him in appreciation. I don't think I could face faking it with those two at a restaurant.

I no longer need to check with the police about the break in since Duke came clean. I check in with Culebra and see how things are progressing with Janet.

He answers on the first ring. His greeting is cheerful, and in the background, I hear music—60s rock and roll.

"Do I hear a juke box?"

He laughs. "Yes. I know, I know. Anna, you won't believe the change in this place. When are you coming to visit us? Adelita and Jane can't wait for you to see their work on the bar."

"Sounds like it's more than the bar that's changed. You sound happy." Even to my ears, my words come out more cynical than approving. I give a mental thump on the head. "Forget I said that. I am really happy that you're happy."

If Culebra notices my skepticism, he pretends not to. "Anna, I haven't felt this in a long time. You've nothing to apologize for. Because of you, I found Jane."

He found Jane? He talks like the hero in a romance novel. I give myself another thump to keep from making some snippy remark. I draw a deep breath.

"I'll be down in a few days. I may bring Frey. He won't believe me if I just tell him what's happening."

"You're always welcome." There's a pause. "Jane is waving from across the room. I'd better go see what she needs. See you soon?"

I barely answer affirmatively before the call is cut and I'm staring at my phone.

It's ten minutes before Frey, David, and Duke return. Frey and I retire to the veranda where I dispatch my sandwich to the seagulls without David and Duke seeing.

When we return, Duke is getting off the phone. "There'll be a workman out tonight to fix the slider. One of us will have to be here."

Frey speaks up without hesitation. "You three go ahead. I'll stay."

"You're okay with that?" I ask.

He nods. "I need to call John-John anyway." He pecks me

on the cheek. "Kitty knows you. It makes sense for me to stay."

We pile into Duke's Escalade and head for Del Mar. We're almost at Kitty's before I ask "How are we handling this?"

I'm riding shotgun, and Duke reaches across me to open his glove box. He retrieves a revolver. "Head on," he says, hefting the gun. "She'll confirm or deny what we know. We'll get the truth. You two carrying?"

David and I nod.

"Good. Here we are."

We pull into Kitty's driveway as the sun sets. Duke kills the lights at the gate. Her house glows with lights both from within and around the property. We leave the car and walk.

The curtains are all open. There's no movement from inside.

Duke gestures to me. "Go around back."

I slip away from the men and head toward the rear of the house. When we were here before, I did not have a chance to see the backyard. There's no fence, and the rear, like the front, is well lit. There's a patio area, a pool and a garden set farther back.

I move cautiously to the French doors open to the evening air. All I hear is the muted clinking of utensils against dishes. When I think it's safe, I peek around. The doorbell rings, and a chair scrapes back. Heavy footsteps move toward the front. It's my chance to step inside.

Kitty's eyes widen when she spots me. She's tied, hands and feet to a chair, at the table. I put my finger to my lips and listen for Duke and David at the front door.

There's no conversation, just the rapid tread of someone running back to the kitchen. He hesitates when he realizes the gun he left beside the single table setting is gone and in my hand. He stops.

"Sit," I say, then call out, "David. Duke. If the front door is locked, come around back. I think I found who we're looking for."

Duke recognizes him right away. "He's the one," he says. "The one who killed Taylor in my office."

The guy remains motionless, eyes darting from one of us to the other. David puts a hand on his shoulder and forces him into a chair. While he handcuffs him, I release Kitty.

She sags with relief. "Thank God. He was going to kill me."

Duke doesn't seem convinced. "Who is he, Kitty?"

She's rubbing feeling back into her wrists. "I swear to God, Duke, I don't know. He broke in one night about a week ago and I've been a prisoner ever since."

I narrow my eyes at her. "You went to see Lorraine after she left the half-way house. She said you're the one who told her to get close to Duke. Why would you?"

Kitty pales. "Yes, I did. I'm not proud of it, but I knew she and Howard were having an affair. When he disappeared, I figured it had something to do with his bookie and his money. I knew he was stealing from Duke. He admitted that." She turns to Duke, hands outstretched. "Duke, you know how Howard left me. I needed money. Before I found out he was dead, I thought if I convinced Lorraine to work with me, we could find out what he was doing with—"

"With the money he stole from me?" Duke's tone is harsh. "You could have come to me. I would have helped you."

Kitty looks away, color flooding her face. "I didn't think you would once you realized what Howard was doing. And," she adds, "I swear to God, I didn't know we were talking about so much money."

Duke doesn't look convinced, but Kitty's words ring true to me. I turn to the guy in the chair. "Who is this?"

David stands behind him. He pats him down, then reaches into the pocket of his jeans. He pulls out a cell phone from one pocket and a wallet from another. He hands them to me while he completes the search, finding a slim, long-handled knife tucked into a sheath at the guy's right ankle. He lays it on the table.

"That's it," he says, stepping back.

I open the wallet first. No identification, just some cash and an electronic keycard marked with a well-known hotel chain's logo.

I put the wallet and key aside.

I try to access the phone log, but it's secured by a code. I raise an eyebrow at David. "Nothing."

Duke moves beside us. "You killed Taylor in my office and tried to pin it on me. Who are you working for?"

No reaction. Not even a blink of concern.

"Well," Duke holds up the knife taken from him carefully, by the tip. "This looks like a twin to the one you used in my office. If we turn this, and you, into the police, I bet they can match the wound to the weapon. This one would have your fingerprints on it. Pretty damning."

Again, no reaction.

I can see by the expression on Duke's face that his patience is wearing thin. He places the knife on the table and reaches into his jacket for his gun. He holds the revolver and presses upward into the guy's chin. "I swear I'll blow your brains out if you don't start talking. If you think there's a big payday out there for you, you're wrong. The money is gone. You're only going to get a needle for your silence."

The guy blinks up at Duke. "What do I get if I talk?"

Duke grins over at me. "He can talk." He lowers the gun slightly, the muzzle still in contact with the guy's neck. "You killed four people. I can't promise you anything, but I know the right word in the right ear might get your sentence reduced to life."

He snorts. "Not much incentive."

David leans down and puts his face close. "How about this? We put a bullet in you and drop you where the police will find you. The knife that's on you connects you to four murders. Let the police decide who you worked for. As it stands, Duke and I are only two victims of a Ponzi scheme. Lorraine won't say anything. She's in enough trouble as it is. Besides, she still thinks the money's out there somewhere. She's delusional enough to think once she's out of jail, she'll go looking. Genny just wanted a nice payday. There's a round-the-world cruise she's been eyeing, and I wouldn't be a bit surprised if she hasn't already made reservations. Once you—or your body—shows up, the police might just close the file.

They may pursue Oswald, but if he's smart and as innocent as he claims, he'll have records to back him up."

David straightens and looks over at me and Duke. "How does that sound to you? Think it works?"

"Works for me," Duke says. "Ties everything up with a nice big bow."

I know David is not shooting anyone in cold blood—it isn't in him. I'm curious what happens if this guy doesn't fold. A lot of what David said was pure conjecture but held the ring of truth. None of us knew what Lorraine was telling the police, or if Genny will take her new found riches and run. On the other hand, there isn't anything to tie David and Duke to Sullivan or Oswald except that they were taken in like everyone else. They are victims.

No reaction from our prisoner. I take my shot. "The way I see it, we have to get rid of this guy." I pull Duke and David aside and speak just loud enough so he can hear. "He's the last link between Howard, his bookie, and us."

Duke jabs a thumb behind him. "Not the last. There's Kitty, too."

Kitty looks startled at hearing her name. She moves closer and bows her head to listen.

"I don't think Kitty has anything to do with the murders. I don't know how yet, but this guy got wind of the Ponzi scheme and wanted to cash in before it was too late. I haven't a clue how he knew Howard and Sullivan were working together or how he knew they were skimming. He definitely had someone pointing him at the right victims."

Duke nods. "There's only one man left standing: Oswald."

"No," David says. "There's Kitty, too."

"But you found me." Kitty joins us, her hands so tightly clasped, her knuckles were white with frustration. "You saw. I was tied up."

"You could have staged that," David says.

"How?" Kitty's voice is shrill. "How could I possibly know you were coming?"

I list possible scenarios. "Duke, are your phones bugged? Do the cars have tracking devices? Could she hire this guy to follow Howard and us?" I look at David. "We were followed to Sarah Sullivan's, and she ended up dead. First, Taylor, then Sullivan, then Howard and Sullivan's wife. Who did they all have in common? You, Duke, yes, but who else?"

Three pairs of eyes go to Kitty.

She gasps, eyes wide. "You're kidding. You think I orchestrated four deaths? You're going to have a damned hard time proving anything like that because it's not true."

"Okay." Duke turns away with a shrug. "That leaves option one. David, there's a tarp in my trunk. We'd be smarter to kill this guy here and decide where to take him after. As Kitty said, no one can link her to anything going on."

David hefts the lifted gun from the table. "We'll use his weapon. Wipe it clean, put it in his hand. If we drop the body beneath the OB pier, it would be in water just long enough to get rid of any residual DNA we may have accidentally deposited on the body."

Duke nods. "Anna, stay here and make sure Kitty doesn't

call the cops before we can get rid of the body." He looks around. "You can also make sure she cleans up after we leave."

All the time we're talking, the guy in the chair looks from one of us to the other. By now, I expected him to show some emotion, to defend himself. Instead, his expression is calm acceptance—even amusement, as if he's privy to a secret we're too dumb to understand.

David lays the gun down. "Is the car open?" he asks Duke.

Duke takes the fob from his pocket and tosses it to David. "Bring the car to the back," he says. "We won't have to haul the body as far."

David catches the fob mid-air. "Be right back."

I wonder what the fuck we're doing next. I know David won't shoot the guy, but I'm not sure about Duke. He's been through a lot in the last couple of days. Even recouping his money, he isn't the type to let it go.

I approach Kitty. "You aren't going to let this happen, are you?" I ask. "Even if you never get caught, you have to live with five deaths on your conscience."

She grabs my hand. "Anna, I swear to you, I'm not involved in this. I never saw this guy before he broke in, and I sure as hell didn't hire him to kill anybody. I admit, I went to Lorraine. I thought she might hear or see something I could use to get money from Harry. I was desperate. I should have gone to Duke first, but I only went to Lorraine. Now, I'm going to lose my home…"

"That's a damned good performance," a voice from the doorway proclaims. "I sure believe you. What about you, David?"

David sighs and shakes his head. "He was waiting for me outside, behind the car," he says. "It was déjà vu."

The guy in the chair sits up straight. "It's about fucking time. Where have you been?"

Donald jabs David with his gun and waves it at the rest of us. "Anna, Duke, guns, please. On the table."

THIRTY

DUKE AND I PLACE OUR GUNS ON THE TABLE and are waved back.

Donald motions to Kitty. "Untie my friend, please. Slowly and carefully."

Kitty walks woodenly toward the chair where the guy suddenly animates. "I expected you yesterday," he barks. Hands free, he pushes her away and unties his feet. He whirls and backhands her.

Kitty stumbles and falls. Her head hits the corner of a counter and she drops to the floor, silent.

I take a reflexive step toward her, but Donald steps between us. He's handed our guns to his now freed confederate. "Don't. I like you, Anna. I'd hate to kill you before we get better acquainted."

I quake with rage. Vampire is near the surface, and I know I could take this idiot's head off without breaking a sweat. Donald stands so close, I can count the pock marks on his bad skin.

David lunges, but is knocked sideways by a gun whip to his head. Donald grabs his confederate's hand. "Easy, Blake. We aren't through with them yet."

Blake reaches down and shoves David into the chair from which he was freed. He isn't as big as David, but muscular enough to handle the task single-handedly. He uses the same rope to secure David's hands and feet and turns to Duke when he's finished.

"Your turn," he says, crooking a finger. "Right here."

Duke shoots me a look but moves toward the chair. "So, Blake," he says, settling himself. "How'd you get involved with this lowlife?"

He sounds as if he knows Donald. I raise an eyebrow. "You know this guy?"

Duke grunts as Blake pulls knots tight around his wrists and ankles. "Oh yeah. Donald Smith. Small time hood. Ran numbers for Sullivan, right? He'd never let you in on anything big."

"Sullivan didn't," I say, recalling our conversation at the estate. "Donald eavesdropped. That's how he knew about Howard's part in the skim. Makes sense you need someone like Blake to do your dirty work. You'd never have the guts to—"

Donald moves faster than I anticipate. He slaps me hard across the face, but I grab his arm and twist.

Blake is at his side before Donald's scream dies away. I should hold back, but vampire is too close. I have Blake's hand in one of mine, and his wrist bent back, bone breaking.

His cries merge with Donald's.

I stop myself from ripping David's bonds free. I shake with impatience as I untie the knots first from him and then from Duke.

Both men look at me with shock and amazement.

I hold up a hand to forestall the barrage of questions they want to ask. "Kitty needs help."

I'm at her side as she regains consciousness. From the corner of my eye, I see Duke and David gathering weapons from the floor. Donald and Blake cradle useless arms, the fight gone from both of them. I put two chairs back to back, seat them, and run a rope around both their torsos.

I turn my attention to Kitty, who struggles to sit up.

"Easy," I say. "You might have a concussion."

She presses a hand to her forehead. "I think I'm okay. Just woozy."

I help her into a chair.

"What happened?" she asks, eyeing Blake and pointing to Donald. "Who's he?"

Duke fills her in, piecing the puzzle together as he goes. "Donald, here, overheard a conversation between Howard, Taylor, and Sullivan. He picked up enough to know there was a lot of money involved. Lorraine was at that same meeting, but when Howard turned up dead, she went on her own hunt for the money while Donald enlisted the help of Blake here. You contacted Lorraine and told her to follow me, someone she'd have known nothing about if you hadn't interfered."

His tone was equal parts reproach and anger. Kitty met his gaze. "I'm sorry," she said. "I didn't mean to put you in danger."

Duke snorts. "Anyway, Donald gets Blake to bring Taylor to my office where he kills him to frame me." He switches his gaze to Donald. "With me out of the way charged with murder, you could focus on Howard, someone I'm sure you saw as the weak link. Was that your thinking?"

Donald looks away, mouth drawn in a thin line.

Duke waves a hand. "No matter. You went after the wrong guy. Howard didn't know what Sullivan did with the money. Sullivan didn't give it up so you killed two men and got nothing. That's when you thought the widow might be of help."

Duke sighs and shakes his head. "You killed her for nothing, too. That story about seeing Lorraine outside her apartment? That was a lie. Lorraine was working with Kitty by then, and when they found out Sullivan contacted me, she became my new best friend. In the meantime, David found the PO box key and got the first of the envelopes. If you were smart, you would have tailed Anna and David instead of trying to find me. But you've never been very smart, have you, Donald?"

No answer.

I release a breath. "We can turn them over to the police and tell them what happened, but I don't know if there's proof to tie Blake to the murders, let alone Donald."

"What about the knife?" Duke points to the knife he took from Blake. "It's identical to the one he used on Taylor. That should be enough to get the investigation started. I can identify him as coming to my office with Taylor. If we're lucky, he used the same weapon on Howard, Sullivan, and Sarah. There's bound to be some DNA—you can't clean a knife thoroughly enough to destroy all blood evidence."

Donald snorts. "You have Blake, sure enough. Not me. You can't prove I did anything."

Blake struggles against his bonds. "Are you fucking kidding me? I'll tell them everything. I'll make sure you go down right alongside me."

"Evidence," Donald answers quietly. "You have no evidence."

Blake stills. He draws a deep breath and lunges backward. As the chairs topple over, he hooks his good arm around Donald's throat and yanks his head to the side.

I'll never forget the sound of Donald's neck breaking.

———◆●◆———

By the time David, Duke, and I are released by the police, it's almost dawn. I called Frey earlier in the evening and told him to go home.

None of us know what Blake will say to the police. He lawyered up immediately. We witnessed him killing Donald, but the knife we took off Blake is the only thing to connect him to Taylor's death. As for Howard, Sullivan, and Sarah, we could only hope there was enough DNA evidence to implicate him in those deaths as well.

A very unsatisfying conclusion.

Duke is in high spirits when he drops David and me off at the office. No one will ever know he recovered the money he and David invested. Lorraine and Kitty knew Duke had some of it, but sharing that information would embroil them in a messy murder investigation. For now, that secret seems safe.

Frey meets me at the door when I pull up. I'm so tired, I promise to fill him in after I sleep and head right for bed. I don't bother to undress or brush my teeth—I just kick off my shoes and slip between the sheets. I think I'm out before my head hits the pillow.

THIRTY-ONE

DAY TWELVE

"ANNA? ANNA, WAKE UP."

At first, I think I'm dreaming and ignore the persistent, irritating buzz in my ear.

"Anna. I'm sorry, honey, but you have to get up."

I use both hands and push. "Go away."

Frey grabs my hands. "Anna. It's Culebra. It's important."

My eyes pop open. "Culebra?"

"Something's happened at Beso. You need to get down there."

He hands me my cell phone. I take it. "Culebra?"

He draws a shaky breath. "Anna. It's Adelita and Janet. They're gone."

His voice fills me with dread. "What do you mean gone?"

Even through the telephone, I hear the sobs he's fighting. "Chael. He took them."

I hand the phone to Frey. "Tell him I'm on my way."

I've never made the trip in faster time. All the way in, I'm seething at Chael. If he hurts Adelita, I'll kill him.

Culebra meets me as I pull in front of the bar. He's unshaven, his face pale. I hug him. He leans against me for an instant, then pushes away.

"Tell me what happened."

He sinks into a bench in front of the newly painted bar. "Chael came here two days ago. He seemed fine, even paid to feed. I didn't realize until too late that he drained the host. He had three vampires with him and all three bodies left behind. When I confronted him, he turned. He chased everybody, vamps and mortals, out and threatened if they ever came back, they'd be killed, too. It was a warning, he said, to turn the bar back to a place for vampires to feed, nothing else."

"What about Adelita? Janet?"

Culebra presses his hands against his eyes. "He took them when he left. Said it was insurance that I'd do what he wanted. Said he'd bring them back in twenty-four hours, but it's been two days and no word."

I grab his hand. "Why didn't you call me right away?"

"I tried, but your phone goes to voicemail. I finally found Frey's number."

Shit. Once again, I forgot to charge that damn cell. I pull him into a hug. "I'm so sorry. I promise, I'll get them back. Does Janet have a cell phone?"

Culebra nods. "She doesn't answer."

I hold out my hand. "Give me your phone. I have a contact in the police department who will put a trace on her number."

Culebra pulls out his phone, and I dial. My hands are shaking. I wish I'd to put an end to Chael a long time ago. If he's hurt one hair on Adelita's head—

The phone traces to a motel in Chula Vista. We jump into Culebra's battered Ford Expedition. If Chael is with Adelita and Janet, he'll recognize my car. I pause to ask if he has his passport—and to grab Adelita's and Janet's as well. Chael not bothering to bring them ratchets up my anxiety. He never intended to bring them back. How did he get them across in the first place?

It takes forty minutes to reach the motel on Broadway in Chula Vista. It's in a well-populated part of town. I park a block away, and Culebra and I scout it out.

The motel is an old-fashioned, low-slung affair with twelve rooms facing the road. The office has a neon arrow pointing to the door. There are only three cars in the parking lot, so I motion to Culebra to stay hidden while I approach the rooms with a vehicle in front.

The curtains are open in the first room, and there's a young woman lounging on the bed watching television. The second is next door to the first and open curtains show an empty living area. While I watch, a door opens and a middle age, paunchy male comes from the bathroom. He has a towel wrapped around his ample waistline. When he reaches for trousers and drops the towel, I hurry on.

I hear Janet before I reach the last room on the end. She's laughing. I distinguish the sound of three men chuckling, and

Adelita giggling.

The curtains are drawn so it's easy to approach the door unnoticed. I'm sure Chael has vampires guarding Janet and Adelita. I motion for Culebra to join me and let vampire take the lead.

I grab the doorknob and twist it off. The chain is on, but a shoulder thrust separates the links. Culebra races toward Janet and Adelita while I have the three vamps on the floor. I'm eager to tear at their throats, but a restraining hand on my arm pulls me back.

I shake myself to call the human Anna back. I whirl on Janet.

She touches my face. "It's all right. We're unharmed."

Adelita hugs Culebra, whispering calming words in his ear.

Janet helps the vampires to their feet. They're very young, fifteen or sixteen in human years, of Middle Eastern descent, and quaking with fear.

Janet goes to Culebra and he sweeps her into his arms. "Are you all right?"

She nods. "We're fine. Really."

I'm having a hard time gathering my wits. "What's going on, Janet?" I ask when I've regained full control. "Where's Chael?"

Hearing Chael's name, the young vamps shrink. Janet turns to them and holds up a calming hand. "It's all right." She turns back to me. "He left us here with them. He comes back tomorrow and expects they'll have killed us. He'll be in for a surprise." She reaches into her pocket and pulls out her cell phone. "I expect this is how you found us."

I nod. "They didn't take it?"

She shakes her head. "These are three very unsophisticated vampires. Chael brought them over, planning, I suspect, to kill them when they fulfilled their task. They didn't look for a phone, and I left it on, knowing either you or Culebra would track us."

Color floods Culebra's face. "I didn't even think of it," he says with a moan. "If it wasn't for Anna—"

Janet touches his face. "It doesn't matter. We would have been home tomorrow anyway. We came to an understanding with our three captors. We're taking them back to the bar. We'll make sure they're safe. When Chael checks here, we'll be gone. If he comes to the bar," she turns to Culebra, "we'll be ready for him."

I'm still not convinced. "They may be unsophisticated, but they killed three people at the bar."

Once more, Janet comes to their defense. "I'm sure they didn't understand what they did. Chael turned them specifically for this task. They're disposable. We can teach them to feed responsibly. When they're ready, I'll take them to my home in LA and introduce them to the vampires I met when doing my research. They'll have a community to belong to."

They belong to Chael's community, I say to Culebra.

Culebra stares at the vampires with a critical eye. *We should kill them,* he says to me.

As if Janet understood his mental communication to me, she places a hand on his arm. "They're harmless," she says.

Adelita nods. "They've been kind to us. Chael ordered them to tie us to the bed, but they let us go as soon as he left. They brought us food. They're scared to death of Chael. I don't believe they would hurt us."

Culebra and I exchange a glance. I turn to one of the vamps.

Do you know where Chael is?

Answer the question, Culebra says, shaking Janet's hand off his arm and taking a menacing step toward them. *Janet thinks you are harmless, I do not.*

The three look at each other. Culebra made it crystal clear we should kill them. They don't exchange words, but desperation darkens their expression.

One speaks up. *He didn't tell us where he would be.* He digs in a pocket of his jeans and pulls out a cell phone. *We're supposed to call him tomorrow morning after—* He glances over at Janet and Adelita- *after it's done. I swear, we already decided not to kill the woman and her daughter. She was taking us with her back to Beso de la Muerte. She said there was someone who could teach us to feed without killing. We just want to be left in peace.*

His words tumble out. I feel a twinge of jealousy when he refers to Janet and Adelita as mother and daughter. But watching the two of them, arms intertwined, I realize it was an easy mistake to make.

Culebra must have thought so, too, because he didn't correct them.

What do you want to do? I ask him.

He sighs. "Let's get them back to Beso."

Janet squeals and throws her arms around Culebra. She and Adelita herd the vamps out to the car.

Once we are on the way back to the border, I ask Culebra about what I wondered earlier. "How did he manage to get Janet, Adelita, and three Middle Eastern vamps across the border?"

Janet speaks up from the back. "We were hidden in a false panel in the bottom of a produce truck," she says, looking around. "I don't know how we're going to do it this time."

I exchange looks with Culebra. *We could do it if it was the four of us*, I say to him. *The three vamps? Janet and Adelita made it clear they want to give them a chance.*

Culebra, at the wheel, grins and says aloud, "Don't worry. I know the border like the back of my hand."

He travels the main highway until just before the border, then turns onto Monument Road. We continue for some time until we come to a crossroads past one of the border patrol stations. It seems deserted. All the same, I hold my breath until we're safely south into Mexico on a bumpy dirt road.

"How did you find this?" I ask Culebra. The border is more heavily patrolled and barricaded than any time before.

He smiles. "Don't forget, I lived in Mexico all my life." He shoots me a sideways look. "That life hasn't always walked the straight and narrow."

I raise my eyebrows. Indeed. I remember I was shocked to learn Culebra was a drug runner and assassin in his youth for one of Mexico's notorious cartel leaders.

Another lifetime ago.

I settle back in the seat. "What will Chael do when he gets to the motel tomorrow and finds everyone gone?"

He smiles grimly. "I hope he comes looking for them at Beso. We'll be ready."

I nod. Chael and I have a checkered relationship, and I was willing to overlook a lot. I cannot forgive taking Adelita. I don't know what the ramifications will be when I kill him. I should know, being the Chosen One, but it doesn't matter.

I close my eyes. I can think of two other times when I purposefully set out to vanquish another vampire. Neither was easy. The vampire inside me stirs at the memory. Like this time, though, it was necessary.

"Are you thinking about tomorrow?"

Culebra's soft voice breaks my reverie. I glance into the back. Janet and Adelita are asleep, Adelita's head on Janet's shoulders.

"You love them," I say.

"More than I thought possible. I was alone for so long, I gave up having a family. They are a gift. I think it's God's way of saying I'm forgiven. If I lost them—"

I touch his arm. "You won't. I want you to do something for me. When we get back to Beso, you take Adelita and Janet and go. Stay in a hotel and don't come back until I tell you it's safe."

Culebra makes a scoffing noise in the back of his throat. "You can't imagine I'll leave you to face Chael alone."

"I won't be alone. I have his kiddie-vamps with me."

That brings a chuckle. "Kiddie-vamps, indeed, but no,

Anna. We face Chael together. It's my family he's threatening. My fight."

"No. I brought the danger to you when Chael delivered Janet. If I came myself, he would have washed his hands of the whole situation and gone home."

"Don't be too sure." Janet says from the back seat. She settles Adelita more comfortably into a corner and leans forward. "He hated me. He made it clear he wants me dead. The only reason he didn't do it himself is because he's afraid of you, Anna. I don't know what kind of story he would have concocted to explain my death, but he intended to. Maybe he thought he'd blame it on the poor vamps he brought with him. Once they were dead, too, they couldn't point the finger, could they?"

She puts a hand on Culebra's shoulder. "I agree we should get Adelita to someplace safe, but I'm standing with you when the fight comes. I never fought for anything in my life. I can't imagine anything more worthy than my family."

For a second, I flash back to the vain, self-centered hellion I met not two weeks ago. The cynic in me wonders if this new improved Janet is an act. Then I think about the bond she and Adelita have formed. The love I see between them is real.

THIRTY-TWO

AFTER MAKING A CALL, WE DROP ADELITA OFF at the home of a school friend whose parents were delighted to have her visit.

She is not happy. She doesn't know what is happening at Beso, but she doesn't want to leave Culebra and Janet to face it alone. It takes persuading to assure her. I remind her that Culebra and I saved her from far worse than one disgruntled vampire when we rescued her before and now when there is so much more at stake, we'd do it again. In order to do that, we had to make sure she's safe.

"But I helped before," she says. "You may need me to help again."

Culebra takes her hand. "You did help before. You were very brave but the situation was different. If we'd had a way to keep you out of that fight, we would have. What you can do now to help is go to your friend's house. It will give Janet and Anna and I the peace of mind to face Chael and not worry that he may hurt you."

Janet puts an arm around Adelita's shoulders. "We'll be back before you know it," she says.

Adelita turns to me. "You'll take care of them."

I nod.

Her mood hasn't lightened, but she manages a smile. We watch her go inside.

On the way to Beso, I borrow Culebra's phone and call Frey. He has news but I start first. I weigh my words carefully. If I tell him I plan to kill Chael, he will insist on joining. Instead, I make up a story about how Janet and Adelita got lost in the desert, but we now had them back home, and I am staying over for a day or two to visit.

In other words, I lie, again.

He tells me his news.

"John-John's grandmother is out of the hospital," he says. "I'm flying out tonight to bring him home. We should be back in San Diego on Wednesday."

I smack my forehead. Two days. I lied to him for nothing. "Perfect," I say, wishing I'd let him speak first. I shake off my guilt and ask, "Do you want me to call the pilot and arrange the flight?"

"No." In my imagination, I can see him shaking his head. "No bother. I already made commercial reservations, so we're all set." He chuckles. "I see you're calling from Culebra's phone. Forgot yours, huh?"

The *again* hangs in the air.

"I know. I'm hopeless."

My chest tightens, thinking that this may be the last time

I speak with him. "I love you, Frey," I whisper.

There's a pause. "Is everything all right?"

I make myself laugh. "Of course. Can't a wife tell her husband she loves him?"

Another heartbeat passes. "I love you, too, Anna. I always have and I always will."

Something catches in my throat. "Enough of the mush. I can't wait to see you and John-John. At least we still have most of the summer ahead of us to enjoy."

"We do, indeed."

"Tell David I'm taking a couple of days off, will you? I think Tracey will be back the end of the week, too."

He agrees. "Give Culebra my best," he says. "Hurry home, okay?"

"I will." My fingers cross tightly behind my back.

We ring off.

Culebra sends everyone away from Beso and closes the mystical doorway. Anyone coming here will now be stopped and urged to turn around by a force neither physical nor mental, but as impossible to ignore as an iron curtain.

Only the doctor is left. Culebra urges him to stay back in the dark cave corridors and wait until he's called for. Culebra has him take the three young vamps back with him.

Now it's only Culebra, Janet and me.

Janet takes me out back and shows the cabin framework that will be home for her and Adelita. The roof is up, the walls are insulated and painted, and the floor is laid. She takes me from a living room with a fireplace, to a large bedroom with a bath, to a smaller second bedroom with bath.

I'm amazed. "How did you get this done so fast?"

She laughs. "Offer enough money and be amazed how quickly you get things done. Even here." She waves a hand toward the bar. "That's a perfect example."

I turn and look, shaking my head. There's new paint, a new roof, and a wrap-around porch with a bar-b-cue at the end. "It's wonderful."

"I'm so glad Culebra let us spruce up the place."

"Spruce up? It's a brand new bar. Are you sure you're not a witch?"

Culebra comes up behind her and puts his arm across her shoulders. "I wouldn't care," he says. "Let's get inside. I fixed a little dinner." He casts a sideways glance my way. "I'm sorry I don't have anything to offer you."

Since I fed from Frey a few days ago, I tell Culebra I'm fine. The young vamps with the doctor back in the cave drained hosts a day ago and should be all right. When the ordeal with Chael is over, their education can begin.

Culebra sets three places at the bar. His and Janet's plates are piled with salad alongside bowls of chili. My mouth waters at the smell of beef and beans, but the only pleasure I take is drinking from an ice cold Corona he sets before me.

Outside, the sun is setting, casting red and gold across the bar. Spears of light dance atop liquor bottles and crystal decanters. Once Culebra offered only beer, now liquors of all colors and types line the walls.

Culebra and Janet finish their dinner, and I finish my beer. I'm suddenly overcome with fatigue. I only slept a few hours before Frey woke me with Culebra's summons. I yawn widely and stand.

"Where can I sleep for the night?" I ask.

Culebra points to the back, the feeding rooms. "Take your pick. The sheets are clean, and the beds are made. Janet and I will stay up here tonight. We won't let Chael sneak up on us."

I leave them and make my way to the back. I take a room at the front, close to the door. I can let the human Anna get some rest while the vampire stays on high alert.

I wish now I had a change of clothes; it's been two days and I'm feeling funky. I manage a sponge bath in one of the bathrooms and finger-brush my teeth. By the time I stretch out, I'm too tired to care. The last I hear, Culebra and Janet make their way into a bedroom. I'm on that half-asleep, half-awake plateau between dream and reality, and I hear the gentle rustle of love making.

Good for you, Culebra.

———●●●———

Vampire alerts me.

I sit straight up in bed.

The bedside clock reads 5:30.

I strain to hear.

The car is a good distance away.

I swing my legs out of bed.

Culebra meets me in the bar.

"Janet?" I whisper.

"Still asleep."

I nod.

We tiptoe to the door and step onto the porch. Headlights zig-zag a path towards town. I point to the far corner just beyond the bar-b-cue.

Culebra understands and moves away.

I hunker down and watch the car approach. I don't know if Chael will be alone or if he's bringing reinforcements. Amazingly, I don't care. Vampire is here with me, eagerness sending a shiver down my spine. By the whisper of motion from Culebra's hiding place, he's shape-shifting. Culebra means snake, his second identity.

The car stops at the edge of town. Chael sends out thought waves to determine if I'm here. My thoughts are shut tightly down. I see through the murky darkness of twilight that he's alone in the car.

Either an act of bravery or stupid vanity.

He opens the door and steps out, calling my name.

I stand.

He is half concealed by the car door. I don't see what he's hiding until a wooden arrow whistles toward me.

Vampire laughs and snatches it out of the air.

Chael fits another arrow into the bow, but I'm at the car before he can send it flying.

I wrench it out of his hand.

He's startled, but not off guard.

This has been coming for a long time, Anna.

Vampire growls in response.

You think you can take me?

He radiates arrogance. I smile and take a step closer.

"Culebra? Where are you?"

Janet's voice from the porch makes me pause.

Chael whips past me and seizes Janet before I can order her inside.

He bends her backward, exposing her neck to his teeth. His eyes find mine and sparkle with pleasure as his jaws tighten.

I'm faster. I wrench her away and push Chael to the floor. Janet stumbles back.

"Get inside." My voice is neither human nor animal, and the guttural roar sends her back through the door.

I pick up Chael and hurl him into the street. He lands in the path of a giant rattle snake inching towards him. Culebra coils and prepares to strike, his tongue flicking like a pointed dagger toward Chael's head.

No.

The snake pauses, head swiveling toward me.

Protect Janet.

The coils loosen and fall away. A naked Culebra rushes past me up the steps.

Chael and I are alone.

His vampire is older, but I idly wonder how many battles he's fought. He always had minions to do his bidding. He's looks up at me and doesn't seem to grasp that he's alone, that

I'm no longer an ally. He looks like a bemused father the first time his child challenges him.

He sits up and pulls at his jacket. "What happens now?"

His human side comes to the fore. Mine doesn't.

You've gone too far. I can't let this pass.

You aren't serious, he snaps. *After all we've been through together, you challenge me over a human and a shape-shifter?*

I challenge you over family. You've been vampire too long to understand.

You haven't been vampire long enough to understand, he whips back. He waves a hand. *None of this is important. None of this is real. Humans are a food source nothing more. They are here to serve us, to be our nourishment. You made them pets, infused with a sense of dangerous entitlement. One day, we will take our rightful place at the top of the food chain, and those you have infected with this foolish self-worth will rise against us. How can you not see that?*

He gets to his feet. He brushes dust from his coat and pants as he talks.

He inches toward me, and his hand moves to an inside coat pocket. He launches toward me, a wooden stake aimed at my heart.

Instinct takes over. I side-step, pirouetting like a bull fighter. One snap of my jaws dispatches the hand with the stake and it falls to the road in a spray of blood.

His eyes grow wide.

He holds up his arm in defense.

I wrap both my arms around him and grind his body

into mine. I don't know what I'll be exposed to when I sink my teeth into his neck until it snaps and the blood is released. Once I start to feed, I can't stop. I'm only aware of the sensations that flood me as I drink. I see his life in flashes, like slides from a projector. His becoming, his blood lust, his victims he tortured and his victims he loved. They all become the same—fodder to feed the hunger. It never changes. Not for years. Not for centuries. His victims are too numerous to count. I'm awash with agony for them, but I can't stop. I feel no pity for him. He lived the life he chose and he dies the death he deserves.

Blood turns to water. I let his body drop to the ground. It's a husk that slowly returns to a natural state— the remains of a man centuries old, desiccated, skin long gone, and bones so brittle that crumble beneath my touch.

I sink beside the remains. Human Anna is overwhelmed, fatigued beyond feeling. A hand touches my shoulder, and I jump.

Culebra looks down at me. He pulls me to my feet. He's dressed again in the same jeans and t-shirt he wore when we were on the porch.

Janet is behind him. She takes my arm and leads me like a weary child into the bar.

THIRTY-THREE

DAY THIRTEEN
I SLEEP FOR TWENTY-FOUR HOURS.

When I awaken, I find clean clothes, a hair brush, tooth-brush, toothpaste, shampoo, and towels neatly piled on the end of my bed. I don't know where Janet got the clothes. She seems able to work miracles, and I accept them gratefully. After a hot shower, I feel human again—well, as human as I can.

Janet and Culebra are both at the bar when I join. The three young vamps are there, too. They converse in halting English, but it's obvious they are eager to please the couple who saved them.

And to please the vampire that freed them.

They immediately stand when I enter the room.

They bow their heads and touch their hands to their hearts.

It makes me uncomfortable.

Culebra smiles. *They pay tribute to the Chosen One,* he says. *You shouldn't be embarrassed.*

I wave them back into their seats and accept the cup of

coffee Culebra offers me before sitting at the table beside Janet.

She looks me over approvingly. "I got your sizes right."

I glance down at the blue silk blouse and dark slacks. "This is nicer than my usual garb," I say. "Jeans and a tee shirt are also fine."

Culebra rests an arm over Janet's shoulders. "How are you feeling, Anna?"

"Like I wrestled an alligator," I say. "Much better this morning than last."

"You're welcome to stay another night," Janet says. "I understand Frey won't be back until tomorrow, and we're reopening the bar. We'll pick up Adelita and have a real celebratory party."

I smile. "It sounds wonderful, but I want to get the house ready. I've been away for weeks." And I may still need to clean up after Duke's escapade. I was so tired after being released by the police, I didn't notice.

Culebra and Janet exchange a smile—a smile that has a secret.

"Okay," I say. "What aren't you telling me?"

Janet grins. "We'll let you out of this party, but there's one coming up that we expect you, Frey, and John-John to play an important part."

I raise an eyebrow. "Oh?"

Before Janet gets the words out, Culebra regales me with a triumphant, *We're getting married.*

———◆●◆———

Two Weeks Later

John-John dances with impatience. "Come on," he exclaims. "We're going to be late and we can't be late. Adelita said."

Frey gives his son a patient look. "We won't be late, John-John. I promise. Anna is almost ready and—"

"Anna is ready," I say, stepping into the room.

John-John does a double take. "You're in a dress."

I want to run back into the bedroom and change, but Frey's look chases that idea out of my head.

"Wow."

I glance down self-consciously. The dress arrived via post with a note from Janet. It was so long since I wore designer clothes, I forgot how sumptuous silk felt against the skin. She chose a Badgley Mischka sheath, nipped in at the waist and falling just below my knees. The matching heels are higher than I ever wore before, but I know nothing else would set off the dress—and my legs—the way these do.

Remarkable, since the moment we met at her estate, Janet presented herself as casual bordering on frumpy. I can hardly wait to see what she chose as her wedding dress.

John-John pulls me toward the door. Laughing, I let him take the lead. Frey snatches up his suit jacket and my purse, and soon we're all in the car heading for a wedding at Beso de la Muerte.

The day is perfect. Blue sky with enough puffy clouds. We pull up to the bar, stunned by the transformation. Bunting hangs from the porch railings, around the doorway, and from tree branches. Rose bushes, ablaze with brilliant red blooms, were planted in white containers. More roses climb an arch that was set up at the bottom of the steps.

One of the Middle Eastern vamps, dressed in a dark suit and white shirt, acts as valet. He takes the keys from Frey with a slight bow and acknowledges me with the hand-on-heart again.

I nod and sigh self-consciously.

We join the crowd on the porch. Vampires, shapeshifters, and humans mingle in joyful anticipation. For a moment, my heart gives into darkness, thinking of Chael. I have no regrets over killing him, just the regret from not understanding why anyone chooses hate over love.

Adelita comes from inside. She's radiant in a white, off-the-shoulder Mexican peasant blouse with beautiful embroidered flowers and a matching embroidered skirt. She makes a beeline to us and grabs John-John's hand.

"Just in time," she says, pulling him away. She turns and giggles. "Hi! See you in a few minutes."

Frey and I laugh. He hooks an arm through mine and pulls me close. "I didn't get a chance to tell you how beautiful you look," he whispers. "You look happy."

For a startled moment, I realize I am. I stand on tip-toe, pull his head toward me and kiss, shutting out everything around us.

Sweet guitar music swirls the air. I release Frey and we turn to the door.

John-John is there, a basket of rose petals in his hands. He grins and walks slowly down the steps, scattering the petals.

Frey leans toward me. "Did you know about this?"

I shake my head. "He and Adelita must have cooked this up."

"Explains why he was so anxious to get here, doesn't it?"

Adelita is at the doorway, carrying a single red rosebud, a garland of greenery in her hair. She joins John-John and they beam at each other.

Frey squeezes my hand.

Culebra walks out next. He's dressed in all black, a traditional Charro suit with embroidery on the jacket and pants. He reaches out and brushes my hand as he walks by.

My heart swells and my breath catches. Since my becoming, Culebra is one of the constants in my life. He's a friend, a mentor, and a voice of reason when I need it most. He never lost faith in me when I stupidly held his past against him. Through all we've gone through, the highs and the lows, the losses and the gains, he's stood beside me.

I want to throw my arms around him, and I know he feels it. He's watching me, smiling.

The music changes and all eyes move once again to the door.

Janet appears like a vision. Her hair is swept up and away from her face, pinned back with a wreath of roses. Her dress is simple, white lace, body skimming, with a short train. While everyone's eyes are on her, her gaze is on one.

Culebra meets her at the bottom of the porch steps. They embrace before turning to the officiant, a young human priest. The ceremony is short, both exchanging vows they wrote.

Adelita takes her place, standing between them, arms inter-linked. The priest blesses them and declares them a family.

I've never seen a more beautiful ceremony.

I look up at Frey.

Except for the one that united us.

ABOUT THE AUTHOR

JEANNE STEIN IS THE AWARD WINNING, national bestselling author of the Urban Fantasy series, *The Anna Strong Vampire Chronicles* and the *Fallen Siren* Series written as S. J. Harper. She has thirteen full length books to her credit, several novellas, and numerous short stories, including "The Wolf's Paw", reprinted in Hex Publishers' 2015 anthology, *Nightmares Unhinged*.

CPSIA information can be obtained
at www.ICGtesting.com
Printed in the USA
BVHW080753040821
613443BV00003B/386

9 781733 917735